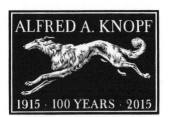

ALFRED A. KNOPF

1915 · 100 YEARS · 2015

ALSO BY HARUKI MURAKAMI

FICTION

1Q84

After Dark

After the Quake

Blind Willow, Sleeping Woman

Colorless Tsukuru Tazaki and His Years of Pilgrimage

Dance Dance Dance

The Elephant Vanishes

Hard-Boiled Wonderland and the End of the World

Kafka on the Shore

Norwegian Wood

South of the Border, West of the Sun

Sputnik Sweetheart

The Strange Library

A Wild Sheep Chase

The Wind-Up Bird Chronicle

NONFICTION

Underground: The Tokyo Gas Attack and the Japanese Psyche

What I Talk About When I Talk About Running: A Memoir

WIND / PINBALL

HARUKI MURAKAMI

TRANSLATED FROM THE JAPANESE BY TED GOOSSEN

TWO NOVELS

WIND / PINBALL

ALFRED A. KNOPF • NEW YORK • 2015

THIS IS A BORZOI BOOK PUBLISHED BY ALFRED A. KNOPF

Translation copyright © 2015 by Haruki Murakami

www.aaknopf.com

Library of Congress Cataloging-in-Publication Data
Murakami, Haruki, [date].
  [Novels. Selections. English]
  Wind/Pinball : two novels / Haruki Murakami ; translated from the Japanese by Ted Goossen.—
First edition.
     pages   cm
  ISBN 978-0-385-35212-3 (hardback)—ISBN 978-0-385-35213-0 (eBook)
  I. Goossen, Ted, translator.   II. Title.
  PL856.U673A2 2015
  895.63'5—dc23

2015010860

Jacket photograph by Geoff Spear
Jacket design by Chip Kidd

Manufactured in the United States of America
First Edition

CONTENTS

THE BIRTH OF

MY KITCHEN-TABLE FICTION

AN INTRODUCTION TO TWO SHORT NOVELS

Most people—by which I mean most of us who are part of Japanese society—graduate from school, then find work, then, after some time has passed, get married. Even I originally intended to follow that pattern. Or at least that was how I imagined things would turn out. Yet in reality I married, then started working, then (somehow) finally managed to graduate. In other words, the order I chose was the exact opposite to what was considered normal.

Since I hated the idea of working for a company, I decided to open my own establishment, a place where people could go to listen to jazz records, have a coffee, eat snacks, and drink. It was a simple, rather happy-go-lucky kind of idea: running a business like that, I figured, would let me relax listening to my favorite music from morning till night. The problem was, since my wife and I had married while still in university, we had no money. Therefore, for the first three years, we worked like slaves, often taking on several jobs at once to save as much as we could. After that, I made the rounds, borrowing whatever money friends and family could spare. Then we took all the funds we had managed to scrape together and opened a small coffee shop/bar in Kokubunji, a student hangout, in the western suburbs of Tokyo. It was 1974.

It cost a lot less to open your own place back then than it does now. Young people like us who were determined to avoid "company life" at all costs were launching small shops left and right. Cafés and restaurants, variety stores, bookstores—you name it. Several places near us were owned and run by people of our generation. Kokubunji retained a strong counterculture vibe, and many of those who hung around the area were dropouts from the shrinking student movement. It was an era when, all over the world, one could still find gaps in the system.

I brought my old upright piano from my parents' house and began offering live music on weekends. There were many young jazz musicians living in the Kokubunji area who happily (I think) played for the small amount we could pay them. Many went on to become well-known musicians; even now I sometimes run across them in jazz clubs around Tokyo.

Although we were doing what we liked, paying back our debts was a constant struggle. We owed the bank, and we owed the people who had supported us. On one occasion, stuck for our monthly payment to the bank, my wife and I were trudging along with our heads down late at night when we stumbled across some money lying in the street. Whether it was synchronicity or some sort of divine intervention I don't know, but the amount was exactly what we needed. Since the payment was due the next day, it was truly a last-minute reprieve. (Strange events like this have happened at various junctures in my life.) Most Japanese would have probably done the proper thing, and turned the money in to the police, but stretched to the limit as we were, we couldn't live by such fine sentiments.

Still, it was fun. No question about that. I was young and in my prime, could listen to my favorite music all day long, and was the lord of my own little domain. I didn't have to squeeze onto packed commuter trains, or attend mind-numbing meetings, or suck up to a boss I disliked. Instead, I had the chance to meet all kinds of interesting people.

My twenties were thus spent paying off loans and doing hard physical labor (making sandwiches and cocktails, hustling foul-mouthed patrons out the door) from morning till night. After a few years, our landlord decided to renovate the Kokubunji building, so we moved to more up-to-date and spacious digs near the center of Tokyo, in Sendagaya. Our new location provided enough room for a grand piano, but our debt increased as a result. So things still weren't any easier.

Looking back, all I can remember is how hard we worked. I imagine most people are relatively laid back in their twenties, but we had virtually no time to enjoy the "carefree days of youth." We barely got by. What free time I did have, though, I spent reading. Along with music, books were my great joy. No matter how busy, or how broke, or how exhausted I was, no one could take those pleasures away from me.

As the end of my twenties approached, our Sendagaya jazz bar was, at last, beginning to show signs of stability. True, we couldn't sit back and relax—we still owed money, and our business had its ups and downs—but at least things seemed headed in a good direction.

.   .   .

One bright April afternoon in 1978, I attended a baseball game at Jingu Stadium, not far from where I lived and worked. It was the Central League season opener, first pitch at one o'clock, the Yakult Swallows against the Hiroshima Carp. I was already a Swallows fan in those days, so I sometimes popped in to catch a game—a substitute, as it were, for taking a walk.

Back then, the Swallows were a perennially weak team (you might guess as much from their name) with little money and no flashy big-name players. Naturally, they weren't very popular. Season opener it may have been, but only a few fans were sitting beyond the outfield fence. I stretched out with a beer to watch the game. At the time there were no bleacher seats there, just a grassy slope. The sky was a sparkling blue, the draft beer as cold as could be, and the ball strikingly white against the green field, the first green I had seen in a long while. The Swallows' first batter was Dave Hilton, a skinny newcomer from the States, and a complete unknown. He batted in the lead-off position. The cleanup hitter was Charlie Manuel, who later became famous as the manager of the Cleveland Indians and the Philadelphia Phillies. Then, though, he was a real stud, a slugger the Japanese fans had dubbed "the Red Demon."

I think Hiroshima's starting pitcher that day was Yoshiro Sotokoba. Yakult countered with Takeshi Yasuda. In the bottom of the first inning, Hilton slammed Sotokoba's first pitch into left field for a clean double. The satisfying crack when the bat met the ball resounded throughout Jingu Stadium. Scattered applause rose around me. In that instant, for no reason and based on no grounds whatsoever, it suddenly struck me: *I think I can write a novel.*

I can still recall the exact sensation. It felt as if something had come fluttering down from the sky, and I had caught it cleanly in my hands. I had no idea why it had *chanced* to fall into my grasp. I didn't know then, and I don't know now. Whatever the reason, *it* had taken place. It was like a revelation. Or maybe "epiphany" is a better word. All I can say is that my life was drastically and permanently altered in that instant—when Dave Hilton belted that beautiful, ringing double at Jingu Stadium.

After the game (Yakult won, as I recall), I took the train to Shinjuku and bought a sheaf of writing paper and a fountain pen. Word processors and computers weren't around back then, which meant we had to write everything by hand, one character at a time. The sensation of writing felt very fresh. I remember how thrilled I was. It had been such a long time since I had put fountain pen to paper.

Each night after that, when I got home late from work, I sat at my kitchen table and wrote. Those few hours before dawn were practically the only time I had free. Over the six or so months that followed, I wrote *Hear the Wind Sing*. I wrapped up the first draft right around the time the baseball season ended. Incidentally, that year the Yakult Swallows bucked the odds and almost everyone's predictions to win the Central League pennant, then went on to defeat the Pacific League champions, the pitching-rich Hankyu Braves, in the Japan Series. It was truly a miraculous season that sent the hearts of all Yakult fans soaring.

Hear the Wind Sing is a short work, closer to a novella than a novel. Yet it took many months and much effort to complete. Part of the reason, of course, was the limited amount of time I had to work on it, but the greater problem was that I hadn't a clue about how to write a novel. To tell the truth, although I was reading all kinds of stuff—my favorites being nineteenth-century Russian novels and American hard-boiled detective stories—I had never taken a serious look at contemporary Japanese fiction. Thus I had no idea what kind of Japanese novels were being read at the time, or how I should write fiction in the Japanese language.

For several months, I operated on pure guesswork, adopting what seemed to be a likely style and running with it. When I read through the result, though, I was far from impressed. While my book seemed to fulfill the formal requirements of a novel, it was somewhat boring and, as a whole, left me cold. *If that's the way the author feels,* I thought dejectedly, *a reader's reaction will probably be even more negative. Looks like I just don't have what it takes.* Under normal circumstances, it would have ended there—I would have walked away. But the epiphany I had received on Jingu Stadium's grassy slope was still clearly etched in my mind.

In retrospect, it was only natural that I was unable to produce a good novel. It was a big mistake to assume that a guy like me who had never written anything in his life could spin off something brilliant right off the bat. I was trying to accomplish the impossible. *Give up trying to write something sophisticated,* I told myself. *Forget all those prescriptive ideas about "the novel" and "literature" and set down your feelings and thoughts as they come to you, freely, in a way that you like.*

While it was easy to talk about setting down one's impressions freely, actually doing it wasn't all that simple. For a sheer beginner like myself, it was especially hard. To make a fresh start, the first thing I had to do was get rid of my stack of manu-

script paper and my fountain pen. As long as they were sitting in front of me, what I was doing felt like "literature." In their place, I pulled out my old Olivetti typewriter from the closet. Then, as an experiment, I decided to write the opening of my novel in English. Since I was willing to try anything, I figured, why not give that a shot?

Needless to say, my ability in English composition didn't amount to much. My vocabulary was severely limited, as was my command of English syntax. I could only write in simple, short sentences. Which meant that, however complex and numerous the thoughts running around my head, I couldn't even attempt to set them down as they came to me. The language had to be simple, my ideas expressed in an easy-to-understand way, the descriptions stripped of all extraneous fat, the form made compact, everything arranged to fit a container of limited size. The result was a rough, uncultivated kind of prose. As I struggled to express myself in that fashion, however, step by step, a distinctive rhythm began to take shape.

Since I was born and raised in Japan, the vocabulary and patterns of the Japanese language had filled the system that was *me* to bursting, like a barn crammed with livestock. When I sought to put my thoughts and feelings into words, those animals began to mill about, and the system crashed. Writing in a foreign language, with all the limitations that entailed, removed this obstacle. It also led me to discover that I could express my thoughts and feelings with a limited set of words and grammatical structures, as long as I combined them effectively and linked them together in a skillful manner. Ultimately, I learned that there was no need for a lot of difficult words—I didn't have to try to impress people with beautiful turns of phrase.

Much later, I found out that the writer Agota Kristof had written a number of wonderful novels in a style that had a very similar effect. Kristof was a Hungarian citizen who escaped to Neuchâtel, Switzerland, in 1956 during the upheaval in her native country. There she had learned—or been forced to learn, really—French. Yet it was through writing in that foreign language that she succeeded in developing a style that was new and uniquely hers. It featured a strong rhythm based on short sentences, diction that was never roundabout but always straightforward, and description that was to the point and free of emotional baggage. Her novels were cloaked in an air of mystery that suggested important matters hidden beneath the surface. I remember feeling somehow or other nostalgic when I first encountered her work. Quite incidentally, her first novel, *The Notebook,* came out in 1986, just seven years after *Hear the Wind Sing.*

Having discovered the curious effect of composing in a foreign language, thereby acquiring a creative rhythm distinctly my own, I returned my Olivetti to the closet and once more pulled out my sheaf of manuscript paper and my fountain pen. Then I sat down and "translated" the chapter or so that I had written in English into Japanese. Well, "transplanted" might be more accurate, since it wasn't a direct verbatim translation. In the process, inevitably, a new style of Japanese emerged. The style that would be mine. A style I myself had *discovered. Now I get it,* I thought. *This is how I should be doing it.* It was a moment of true clarity, when the scales fell from my eyes.

Some people have said, "Your work has the feel of translation." The precise meaning of that statement escapes me, but I think it hits the mark in one way, and entirely misses it in another. Since the opening passages of my first novella were, quite literally, "translated," the comment is not entirely wrong; yet it applies merely to my process of writing. What I was seeking by writing first in English and then "translating" into Japanese was no less than the creation of an unadorned "neutral" style that would allow me freer movement. My interest was not in creating a watered-down form of Japanese. I wanted to deploy a type of Japanese as far removed as possible from so-called literary language in order to write in my own natural voice. That required desperate measures. I would go so far as to say that, at that time, I may have regarded Japanese as no more than a functional tool.

Some of my critics saw this as a threatening affront to our national language. Language is very tough, though, a tenacity that is backed up by a long history. However it is treated, its autonomy cannot be lost or seriously damaged, even if that treatment is rather rough. It is the inherent right of all writers to experiment with the possibilities of language in every way they can imagine—without that adventurous spirit, nothing new can ever be born. My style in Japanese differs from Tanizaki's, as it does from Kawabata's. That is only natural. After all, I'm another guy, an independent writer named Haruki Murakami.

It was a sunny Sunday morning in spring when I got the call from an editor at the literary journal *Gunzo* telling me that *Hear the Wind Sing* had been short-listed for their new writers' prize. Almost a year had passed since the season opener at Jingu Stadium, and I had turned thirty. It was around 11 a.m., but I was still fast asleep, having worked very late the night before. I groggily picked up the receiver, but I had no idea at first who was on the other end or what he was trying to tell me. To tell the truth, by that time, I had quite forgotten that I had sent off *Hear the Wind Sing* to *Gunzo*. Once I had finished the manuscript and put it in someone else's hands, my desire to write had altogether subsided. Composing it had been, so to speak, an act of defiance—I had written it very easily, just as it came to me—so the idea that it might make the short list had never occurred to me. In fact, I had sent them my only copy. If they hadn't selected it, it probably would have vanished forever. (*Gunzo* didn't return rejected manuscripts.) Most likely too, I would have never written another novel. Life is strange.

The editor told me that there were five finalists, including me. I was surprised, but I was also very sleepy, so the reality of what had happened didn't really sink in. I got out of bed, washed up, got dressed, and went for a walk with my wife. Just when we were passing the local elementary school, I noticed a passenger pigeon hiding in the shrubbery. When I picked it up I saw that it seemed to have a broken wing. A metal tag was affixed to its leg. I gathered it gently in my hands and carried it to the closest police station, at Aoyama-Omotesando. As I walked there along the side streets of Harajuku, the warmth of the wounded pigeon sank into my hands. I felt it quivering. That Sunday was bright and clear, and the trees, the buildings, and the shopwindows sparkled beautifully in the spring sunlight.

That's when it hit me. I was going to win the prize. And I was going to go on to become a novelist who would enjoy some degree of success. It was an audacious presumption, but I was sure at that moment that it would happen. Completely sure. Not in a theoretical way, but directly and intuitively.

I wrote *Pinball, 1973* the following year as a sequel to *Hear the Wind Sing*. I was still running the jazz bar, which meant that *Pinball* was also written late at night at my kitchen table. It is with love mingled with a bit of embarrassment that I call these two works my kitchen-table novels. It was shortly after completing *Pinball, 1973* that I made up my mind to become a full-time writer and we sold the business. I immediately set to work on my first full-length novel, *A Wild Sheep Chase,* which I consider to be the true beginning of my career as a novelist.

Nevertheless, these two short works played an important role in what I have accomplished. They are totally irreplaceable, much like friends from long ago. It seems unlikely that we will ever get together again, but I will never forget their friendship. They were a crucial, precious presence in my life back then. They warmed my heart, and encouraged me on my way.

I can still remember, with complete clarity, the way I felt when whatever it was came fluttering down into my hands that day thirty years ago on the grass behind the outfield fence at Jingu Stadium; and I recall just as clearly the warmth of the wounded pigeon I picked up in those same hands that spring afternoon a year later, near Sendagaya Elementary School. I always call up those sensations when I think about what it means to write a novel. Such tactile memories teach me to believe in that *something* I carry within me, and to dream of the possibilities it offers. How wonderful it is that those sensations still reside within me today.

JUNE 2014

 HEAR THE WIND SING

▶ 1

"There's no such thing as a perfect piece of writing. Just as there's no such thing as perfect despair." So said a writer I bumped into back when I was a university student. It wasn't until much later that I could grasp his full meaning, but I still found consolation in his words—that there's no such thing as perfect writing.

All the same, I despaired whenever I sat down to write. The scope of what I could handle was just too limited. I could write something about an elephant, let's say, but when it came to the elephant's trainer, I might draw a blank. That kind of thing.

I was caught in this bind for eight years—eight years. A long time.

If one operates on the principle that everything can be a learning experience, then of course aging needn't be so painful. That's what they tell us, anyway.

From the age of twenty on, I did my best to live according to that philosophy. As a result, I was cheated and misunderstood, used and abused, time and again. Yet it also brought me many strange experiences. All sorts of people told me their stories.

Then they left, never to return, as if I were no more than a bridge they were clattering across. I, however, kept my lips zipped tight. And so the stories stayed with me until I entered this, the final year of my twenties.

Now I think it's time to tell my story.

Which doesn't mean, of course, that I have resolved even one of my problems, or that I will be somehow different when I finish. I may not have changed at all. In the end, writing is not a full step toward self-healing, just a tiny, very tentative move in that direction.

All the same, writing honestly is very difficult. The more I try to be honest, the farther my words sink into darkness.

Don't take this as an excuse. I promise you—I've told my story as best I can right now. There's nothing to add. Yet I can't help thinking: if all goes well, a time may come, years or even decades from now, when I will discover that my self has been salvaged and redeemed. Then the elephant will return to the veldt, and I will tell the story of the world in words far more beautiful than these.

*

I learned a lot of what I know about writing from Derek Hartfield. Almost everything, in fact. Unfortunately, as a writer, Hartfield was sterile in the full sense of the word. One has only to read some of his stuff to see that. His prose is mangled, his stories slapdash, his themes juvenile. Yet he was a fighter as few are, a man who used words as weapons. In my opinion, when it comes to sheer combativeness he should be ranked right up there with the giants of his day, Hemingway and Fitzgerald. Sadly, however, he could never fully grasp exactly what it was he was fighting against. In the final reckoning, I suppose, that's what being sterile is all about.

Hartfield waged his fruitless battle for eight years and two months, and then he died. In June 1938, on a sunny Sunday morning, he jumped off the Empire State Building clutching a portrait of Adolf Hitler in his right hand and an open umbrella in his left. Few people noticed, though—he was as ignored in death as he had been in life.

I came across a copy of Hartfield's long-out-of-print first book during my last summer vacation of junior high, a time marked in my memory by a terrible case of crotch rot. The uncle who gave me the book died in agony three years later of intestinal cancer. The last time I saw him, the doctors had hacked him up so badly that he bristled with plastic tubes ferrying fluids in and out of both ends of his body. He was shrunken and his skin had turned reddish brown, so that he resembled a crafty old monkey.

*

I had three uncles in total. One died just outside Shanghai two days after the end of the Pacific War when he stepped on a land mine he himself had laid. My sole surviving uncle works as a magician on the Japanese hot springs circuit.

*

Hartfield says this about good writing: "Writing is, in effect, the act of verifying the distance between us and the things surrounding us. What we need is not sensitivity but a measuring stick" (from *What's So Bad About Feeling Good?*, 1936).

I began fearfully scanning the world around me with a measuring stick in hand the year Kennedy was shot, which was fifteen years ago now—fifteen years spent jettisoning one thing after another. Like an airplane with engine trouble, I started by pitching out the cargo, then the seats, then, finally, the poor flight attendants, getting rid of everything while taking on nothing new at all.

Was this the right way? How the hell should I know! Sure, life is easier like this, but I get scared when I imagine what it will be like to be old and facing death. I mean, what will be left after they incinerate my corpse? Not even a shard of bone.

My late grandmother used to say, "People with dark hearts have dark dreams. Those whose hearts are even darker can't dream at all."

The night she died, the first thing I did was reach out and gently close her eyes. And in that moment, all the dreams she'd seen in her seventy-nine years vanished without a sound (poof!), like a summer shower on hot pavement. Nothing left.

*

One last thing about writing.

I find the act of writing very painful. I can go a whole month without managing a single line, or write three days and nights straight, only to find the whole thing has missed the mark.

At the same time, though, I love writing. Ascribing meaning to life is a piece of cake compared to actually living it.

I was in my teens, I think, when I discovered this, and it so completely blew my mind that I couldn't talk for a week. If I could just keep my wits about me, I felt, I could force the world to conform to my will, overturning whole systems of values, and altering the flow of time.

Sadly for me, it took ages to see that this was a trap. When at last I caught on, I took a blank notebook and drew a line down the middle; then I listed all that I had gained from this principle on the left-hand side and all that I had lost on the right. It turned out that I had lost so much—things long abandoned, trampled underfoot, sacrificed, betrayed—I couldn't even write them all down.

A gulf separates what we attempt to perceive from what we are actually able to perceive. It is so deep that it can never be calculated, however long our measuring stick. What I can set down here is no more than a list. It's not a novel or even literature, nor is it art. It's just a notebook with a line drawn down the middle. It may contain something of a moral, though.

If it's art or literature you're interested in, I suggest you read the Greeks. Pure art exists only in slave-owning societies. The Greeks had slaves to till their fields, prepare their meals, and row their galleys while they lay about on sun-splashed Mediterranean beaches, composing poems and grappling with mathematical equations. That's what art is.

If you're the sort of guy who raids the refrigerators of silent kitchens at three o'clock in the morning, you can only write accordingly.

That's who I am.

▸ **2**

This story begins on August 8, 1970, and ends eighteen days later—in other words, on August 26 of the same year.

▸ **3**

"Eat shit, you rich bastards!" the Rat shouted, glowering at me, with his hands resting on the bar.

Maybe it wasn't me he was bellowing at but the coffee grinder behind me. Since we were sitting side by side, he really didn't have to raise his voice like that. Whatever the cause, he seemed to have become his old self again. He took a satisfied swig of beer.

No one in the bar gave a damn about the Rat's shouting. Fact was, the place was so packed everyone and his cousin was yelling. It looked like the *Titanic* just before it sank.

"Leeches!" the Rat spat out, shaking his head. "The bastards can't do a damn thing for themselves. Looking at their faces makes me want to puke."

I nodded back without taking my lips from the rim of my glass. Rant ended, the Rat began contemplating his slender fingers, turning them back and forth on the bar, as if warming them over a fire. I studied the ceiling and waited. He would have to examine each finger before our conversation could resume. So what else was new?

The Rat and I had spent the whole summer as if possessed, drinking enough beer to fill a twenty-five-meter pool and scattering enough peanut shells to cover the entire floor of J's Bar to a depth of two inches. We were bored out of our skulls that summer, and surviving the only way we knew how.

When the boredom grew too much to bear, I contemplated the nicotine-stained print hanging behind the bar. It was the kind of picture you'd find on a Rorschach test: from where I sat, it resembled two green monkeys tossing deflated tennis balls back and forth. I spent hours looking at it.

When I told J the bartender what it reminded me of, he just shrugged. "Yeah, I guess I can see that," he said, after studying it for a moment.

"But what do you think it symbolizes?" I persisted.

"The monkey on the left is you," he replied. "And the one on the right is me. I'm throwing you a beer and you're tossing me back the money."

Far out, I thought, taking another swig of beer.

"Makes me want to puke," said the Rat, his finger inspection complete.

The Rat was always running down the rich—he out-and-out despised them. Yet his family was loaded. Whenever I pointed that out, his reply was always, "Ain't my fault." There were times (usually when we were smashed) when I said, "Sure it is," but to say that only bummed me out. I knew there was some truth in what he said.

"Know why I hate the rich so much?" the Rat continued. This was the first time he'd gotten past the puking part.

I shook my head no.

"To be blunt, 'cause they don't have a goddamn clue. They can't scratch their own asses without a flashlight and a measuring tape."

"To be blunt" was one of the Rat's signature phrases.

"Oh yeah?"

"Yeah. They're totally in the dark, the whole lot of them. They only pretend to think about important stuff . . . Know why?"

"No, why?"

"'Cause they don't need to, that's why. Sure, they have to use their brains a little to get rich in the first place, but once they make it, it's a piece of cake—they don't need to think anymore. Like an orbiting satellite doesn't need gas. They just keep going round and round, always over the same damn place. But I'm not like that, and neither are you. We have to use our brains to survive. We think about everything, from tomorrow's weather to the size of the bathtub plug. Right?"

"Right," I said.

"That's where things stand."

The Rat looked bored. He pulled out a tissue and blew his nose. He'd said everything he wanted to say, but how seriously was I supposed to take him? I had no idea.

"In the end we all die anyway," I said, trying to feel him out.

"Yeah. We all die. But it'll take another fifty years. And, to be blunt, fifty years spent thinking is a helluva lot more exhausting than five thousand years of living without using your brain, right?"

No argument there.

▸ **4**

I had met the Rat three years earlier. It was the spring of our first year in college, and both of us were flat-out wasted. In fact, for the life of me, I can't remember how we met or how I ended up in his shiny black Fiat 600 at 4 a.m. Maybe we had a mutual friend.

Anyhow, there we were, smashed, flying down the road. Which explains why we went merrily crashing through the park fence, bulldozed the azaleas, and wrapped ourselves around one of the stone pillars. It was a frigging miracle neither of us got hurt.

When I recovered from the shock, I kicked my way out through the busted car door and surveyed the damage. The front grill had assumed the exact shape of the pillar, while the hood had flown off and landed some ten yards away, in front of the monkey cage. Judging by the sounds they were making, the monkeys did not appreciate being awoken in such a rude fashion.

With both hands still on the wheel, the Rat was bent over vomiting the pizza he'd eaten an hour before all over the dashboard. I scrambled up onto the car and looked down at him through the sunroof.

"Are you okay?" I called to him.

"Yeah, but I guess I overdid the booze. Puking like this."

"Can you get out?"

"Yeah. Just give me a boost."

The Rat cut the engine, stuck the pack of cigarettes he'd left on the dashboard into his pocket, grabbed my hand, and calmly climbed up onto the car roof. There we sat side by side, smoking one cigarette after another in silence as the sky began to lighten. For some reason, I started thinking about a Richard Burton war movie, that one where he plays a tank commander. I have no idea what was on the Rat's mind.

"Hey," he said after about five minutes. "We're a lucky pair, don't you think? I mean, just look at us—not a scratch. Can you believe it?"

I nodded. "But the car's a write-off," I said.

"Don't sweat it. I can always buy a new one. But you can't buy luck."

I gave the Rat a closer look. "Are you rich or something?"

"Looks like it."

"That's good."

The Rat shook his head in disgust. "Whatever. But at least we've got luck on our side."

"Yeah, you're right."

The Rat ground out his cigarette with the heel of his sneaker and flicked the butt toward the monkey cage.

"Hey, how about we team up? We could have a blast."

"What should we do now?"

"Drink more beer."

We bought a half-dozen cans from a nearby vending machine and carried them down to the ocean, lay on the beach, and drank. When we'd drained them all we just looked at the water. The weather was perfect.

"You can call me Rat," he said.

"How'd you get a name like that?"

"Don't remember. Happened a long time ago. It bugged me at first, but not anymore. A guy can get used to anything."

We chucked the empty cans into the ocean, propped our backs against the embankment, pulled our coats over our heads, and took an hour-long nap. When I woke I was filled with an intense sense of being alive. It was weird—I had never felt that kind of energy before.

"Man, I feel like I could run sixty miles!" I told the Rat.

"Me too," he said.

But what we had to do in reality was make payments over the next three years, with interest, to city hall for the cost of repairing the damage to the park.

▸ 5

The Rat is a virtual stranger to books. In fact, the only things I've seen him read are sports newspapers and junk mail. Still, he's always curious about the books I read to kill time, peering at them with the curiosity of a fly staring at a flyswatter.

"Why do you read books?" he asked.

"Why do you drink beer?" I replied without glancing in his direction, taking alternate mouthfuls of pickled herring and green salad. The Rat saw this as a very serious question.

"The good thing about beer," he said about five minutes later, "is that you piss it all out. Like a one-out, one-on double play, nothing's left over."

He studied me as I ate.

"So why do you read books all the time?" he asked again.

I washed down the last piece of herring and set the plate aside. Then I picked up my copy of *A Sentimental Education* and flipped through the pages.

"It's because Flaubert's already dead."

"So you don't read books by living writers?"

"No, I don't see the point."

"Why not?"

"I guess because I feel like I can forgive dead people," I said, shifting my attention to the *Route 66* rerun on the portable TV behind the bar. "As a rule, that is." That sent the Rat back to thinking.

"So then what about people who are alive and breathing?" he said a few minutes later. "As a rule, you can't forgive them?"

"I wonder. Haven't given it much thought. But if you backed me into a corner then I'd have to say, yeah, it's possible. Maybe I can't forgive them."

J came and set two fresh beers on the counter in front of us.

"So then what would you do?"

"I'd go to bed and hug my pillow," I answered.

"That's too weird for me," the Rat said, shaking his head.

I poured beer in the Rat's glass, but he just sat there hunched over, lost in thought.

"The last book I read was last summer," he said presently. "Can't remember the title or the author's name. Forget why I read it, too. Anyway, it was by a woman. The main character is this fashion designer, a woman about thirty, who's obsessed with this idea that she's got an incurable disease."

"What kind of incurable disease?"

"I dunno, maybe cancer. Is there any other kind? . . . So she goes to a seaside resort where she spends all her time masturbating. In the bath, in the woods, on the bed, in the ocean, that's all she does, masturbates everywhere you can imagine."

"In the ocean?"

"Yeah . . . Can you believe it? Why would anybody put that in a novel? There's plenty of other things to write about, right?"

"You'd think so."

"A novel like that's not for me. Makes me want to puke."

I nodded.

"If it were my novel, I'd do it differently."

"Like how?"

The Rat fiddled with the rim of his glass and thought.

"Okay, how about this? I'm on a boat in the middle of the Pacific, see, and it sinks. So I grab a life preserver, and there I am floating around in the water all by myself, looking up at the stars. It's a beautiful, quiet night. And then I see this young woman paddling toward me, clinging to her own life preserver."

"Is she hot?"

"You bet."

I took a sip of my beer.

"Sounds pretty lame," I said, shaking my head.

"Hold on, I'm not done. So then the two of us start talking, floating right there in the middle of the ocean. We talk about all kinds of stuff—the past and the future, our hobbies, how many girls I've slept with, what TV shows we like, what we dreamed the night before, that sort of thing. Then we start drinking beer."

"Wait a minute there. Where does the beer come from?"

The Rat thought for a moment. "It's drifting in the water," he said. "Cans of beer that floated out from the ship's kitchen. Cans of sardines, too. Does that work?"

"Okay."

"After a while it grows light. 'What'll you do now?' the girl asks. 'I've got a hunch an island is nearby; I think I'll swim in that direction.' But I know her hunch may be wrong. So I tell her, 'Let's just keep floating here and drinking beer. An airplane is sure to come and rescue us in the end.' But she swims off alone."

The Rat sighed and took a swig of beer.

"She swims for two days and two nights and finally reaches an island. True to form, I've got a major hangover by the time the airplane finds me. Then, years later, the two of us bump into each other in a little neighborhood bar."

"And you start drinking beer again, right?"

"Doesn't it make you want to cry?"

"Yeah, sure," I said.

▸ 6

The Rat's novel had two good things about it. First, there were no sex scenes; second, no one died. Guys don't need any encouragement—left to themselves, they still die and sleep with girls. That's just the way it is.

*

"Do you think I was wrong?" the girl asks.

The Rat takes another swig of beer. "To be blunt," he says, slowly shaking his head, "we're all wrong, every one of us."

"Why do you think that?"

The Rat sighs and licks his upper lip. There's no way to answer her.

"I swam and swam toward that island until I thought my arms would fall off. It hurt so much I thought I would die. And you know what I kept thinking as I swam? That maybe you were right and I was wrong. I kept asking myself, how could you just float there not doing anything when I was suffering?"

The girl gives a small, sad laugh and presses the corners of her eyes with her fingertips. The Rat squirms and fishes about in his pockets. Three years without a cigarette, but now he's got to have one.

"Did you wish I were dead?"

"A little."

"Really just a little?"

". . . I forget what I felt."

They both fall silent. The Rat senses the need to say something.

"All men are not created equal, you know."

"Who said that?"

"John F. Kennedy."

▸ 7

I was a very quiet child. So quiet, in fact, that my worried parents took me to see a friend of theirs who was a psychiatrist.

This doctor's house was perched on a bluff overlooking the ocean. I sat on his sofa in a bright, sunlit drawing room while an elegant middle-aged lady served me cold orange juice and two doughnuts. I drank the juice and ate half of one of the doughnuts, taking care not to spill any of the sugar on my knees.

"Want some more juice?" the doctor asked. I shook my head. Just the two of us were there, sitting face-to-face. On the opposite wall hung a portrait of Mozart. He glared at me in reproach, like a timid cat.

"Long ago," began the doctor, "there lived a friendly goat." It was a great opening. I closed my eyes and imagined a friendly goat.

"The goat carried a heavy gold watch on a chain around his neck that made him huff and puff when he walked. Not only was this watch an awful burden, its hands no longer moved. One day, the rabbit, a friend of the goat, came to see him. 'Why lug that useless watch around everywhere?' he asked the goat. 'It doesn't work, and it looks very heavy.' 'You're right, it is heavy,' answered the goat. 'But I've grown used to it. To its weight, and the fact that its hands don't move.'"

The doctor took a sip from his own glass of orange juice and smiled at me. I sat there and waited for him to continue.

"One afternoon, on the friendly goat's birthday, the rabbit showed up carrying a small box tied with a beautiful ribbon. Inside was a glittering, lightweight new watch in perfect working order. The goat happily hung the watch from his neck and ran around to show it to all of his friends."

The story abruptly broke off there.

"You are the goat," said the doctor. "I am the rabbit, and the watch is your heart."

I felt helpless, as if I had been tricked. All I could do was nod.

After that we began meeting every Sunday afternoon. I had to take a train and then a bus to reach the doctor's home, where, each visit, I was treated to muffins, apple pie, syrupy pancakes, honeyed croissants, and other sweets. These treatments lasted a whole year, after which I was stuck paying regular visits to the dentist.

· · ·

"Civilization is communication," the doctor said. "That which is not expressed doesn't exist. Understand? A big fat zero. Let's say you want something to eat. All you need to do is say the words, 'I'm hungry.' Then I give you cookies. Go ahead, take them. [I grabbed a cookie.] If you don't speak, then there are no cookies. [As if to be mean, the doctor snatched the plate of cookies and hid it under his desk.] Zero. Got it? You don't want to talk. But you're hungry. So you want to tell people without using words. Like a game of pantomime. Try it."

I grabbed my stomach and made a painful face. The doctor laughed. "You look like you've got a stomachache," he said.

A stomachache . . .

We went on from there to free association.

"Say something about a cat. Anything."

I slowly rotated my head, pretending to be thinking.

"Whatever comes to mind."

"It has four legs."

"So does an elephant."

"It's a lot smaller."

"What else?"

"It lives in people's homes and kills mice when it feels like it."

"What does it eat?"

"Fish."

"How about sausages?"

"Sausages too."

We carried on in that vein.

The doctor was right. Civilization is communication. When that which should be expressed and transmitted is lost, civilization comes to an end. Click . . . OFF.

In the spring of my fourteenth year, without warning, a torrent of words came gushing from my mouth. It was as if a dam had broken. I have no memory of what I said, but for the next three months I talked nonstop, as if trying to fill in the void of the previous fourteen years. When the flood of words ended in mid-July, I developed a high fever and had to stay home from school for three days. Once the fever subsided, I was no longer a chatterbox, nor was I tongue-tied. I was just an ordinary kid.

▸ **8**

I woke before 6 a.m. feeling very thirsty. Whenever I wake up in someone else's home, I feel like I'm stuck in another body inhabited by someone else's spirit. It took every ounce of energy just to drag myself out of the narrow bed and walk to the sink by the door, where I drank like a horse, draining glass after glass of water before staggering back to bed.

Through an open window, a thin slice of ocean was visible, its ripples glittering in the early-morning sun. If I looked hard I could make out several grimy, tired-looking freighters floating far offshore. All signs pointed to another scorcher of a day. The whole neighborhood was asleep, the only sounds the occasional creak of the train tracks and the faint melody of a radio calisthenics broadcast.

Still naked, I propped myself against the headboard, lit a cigarette, and studied the girl lying beside me. Since the window faced south, her whole body was in direct sunlight. She was sound asleep with the terry-cloth blanket pushed down to her ankles. Every so often her breath would quicken, and her well-shaped breasts would rise and fall. She had a deep tan, but the sheen had dulled with time, and the white patches left by her swimsuit looked almost rotten.

I finished my smoke and then wasted the next ten minutes attempting to recall her name. The problem was I couldn't remember if she'd mentioned it in the first place. Giving up, I yawned and took another look at her body. She was on the skinny side, probably a year or two shy of twenty. Using my open hand, I measured her from head to toe. Eight hand lengths, with a thumb left over for her heel. It added up to precisely five feet three inches.

There was a coin-sized mark the color of Worcestershire sauce below her right breast. Her delicate pubic hair reminded me of river grass after a flood. To top things off, her left hand had only four fingers.

▸ 9

It took her about three hours to wake up and another five minutes to become aware of her surroundings. All that time I sat there with my arms folded, watching the thick clouds on the horizon change shape as they headed east.

The next time I checked, she had pulled her terry-cloth blanket up to her neck and was looking up at me with a vacant expression. She seemed to be fighting the fumes of what whiskey remained in her belly.

"Who . . . are you?"

"You don't remember?"

She gave a quick shake of her head. I lit a cigarette and offered her one, which she ignored.

"Explain."

"Where should I begin?"

"At the beginning."

The beginning? I hadn't a clue where that was, or how to explain things in a way she could accept. It might work, but then again it might not. It took me ten seconds to put my thoughts in order.

"It was a balmy day," I began. "I spent the afternoon swimming at the pool, then went home, took a nap, and had dinner. By then it was after eight. I got in my car and went for a drive. I stopped along the coast road and looked at the ocean while listening to the radio. It's a habit of mine.

"After about half an hour of that I started feeling like I wanted some company. Looking at the ocean makes me miss people, and hanging out with people makes me miss the ocean. It's weird. Anyway, I decided to go to J's Bar. A cold beer was calling me, and I figured my buddy would be there. He wasn't, though. So I drank alone. Three beers in just an hour."

I broke off to flick my ash into the ashtray.

"By the way, did you ever read *Cat on a Hot Tin Roof*?"

She didn't reply, just lay there glaring at the ceiling and clutching her blanket like a beached mermaid. No big deal. I went on with my story.

"See, I always think of that play when I'm drinking alone. As if I'll reach a moment when something will click in my head and all my problems will disappear. But it never works that way. Nothing ever clicks. Anyway, after a while I got tired of waiting for my buddy, so I phoned his apartment. Figured I'd invite him out for a few drinks. But a girl answered the phone . . . Freaked me out. I mean, he's not that kind of guy. There could be fifty girls there with him totally sloshed, but he'd still answer his own phone. Know what I mean?

"I pretended I'd dialed the wrong number and hung up. Still, the call made me feel kind of low. Don't know why exactly. So I had another beer. But it didn't cheer me up. Sure, I was acting like an idiot. But, hey, what else is new? I finished my beer and called J over so I could pay my tab. Figured I'd head home, listen to the baseball scores, and go to bed. But he tells me to go to the washroom and wash my face. J believes you can drink a case of beer and still drive as long as you splash water on your face first. So I head off in the direction of the washroom. To tell you the truth, though, I wasn't really planning to wash up. I was just going to fake it. J's sink is usually backed up, with water in the basin. I don't like going in there. But last night, for a change, the sink was fine. But you were sprawled out on the floor."

She sighed and closed her eyes.

"And then?"

"Then I hoisted you off the washroom floor and lugged you back to the bar, figuring I could find someone who knew you. But no one did. Then J and I patched up your wound."

"Wound?"

"You whacked your head when you fell. Just a little cut."

Nodding, she drew her hand from the blanket and passed it across the cut on her forehead.

"So J and I talked it over. To decide what to do about you. In the end, I brought you home in my car. We went through your bag and came up with a change purse, a key holder, and a postcard with your name and address on it. I took money from the change purse to pay your tab, drove to the address on the postcard, and used your key to let us in. Then I put you to bed. End of story. The receipt for the bar bill is in your purse."

She took a deep breath.

"So why did you crash here?"

"?"

"Why didn't you just take off once you'd put me to bed?"

"A friend of mine died of alcohol poisoning. He chugged some whiskey, said goodbye, walked home, brushed his teeth, put on his pajamas, and went to bed. Next morning he was stone cold. Fine funeral, though."

". . . You mean to say you nursed me all night?"

"I planned to head home around four. But I fell asleep. I thought of leaving when I woke up too. But I decided to hang around."

"Why?"

"I figured you should at least know what happened."

"A real gentleman, huh?"

Her words were as poisonous as she could make them. I shrugged and let them pass. Then I went back to watching the clouds.

"Did I . . . say anything?"

"A little."

"Like what?"

"Like a few things. I've forgotten what. No big deal."

She groaned without opening her eyes.

"The postcard?"

"It's in your bag."

"Did you read it?"

"Give me a break."

"Why not?"

"Why would I?"

I was getting fed up. Something about her tone pissed me off. At the same time, though, I have to admit she was making me feel a little nostalgic. For something in the distant past. If we'd had the good fortune to meet under more normal circumstances, we might have spent our time together more pleasantly. Or so it felt. Yet for the life of me I couldn't remember what it was like to meet a girl under normal circumstances.

"What time is it?" she asked.

Somewhat relieved, I got out of bed and checked the electric clock on her desk, then filled a glass with water and brought it back to her.

"Nine o'clock."

She gave a weak nod, sat up, and drained the glass with her back against the wall.

"Did I drink a lot?"

"Quite a bit. I would have died."

"I feel half dead right now."

She took a cigarette from the pack next to the bed, lit it, and let out a sigh with the first puff. She flipped the match out the open window toward the harbor.

"Grab me something to wear."

"Like what?"

She closed her eyes again, the cigarette still dangling from her lips. "Any old thing. And cool it with the damn questions."

I went to the wardrobe across the room, opened the doors,

and, after some hesitation, took out a sleeveless blue shift and handed it to her. She pulled it over her head without bothering to put on panties, and zipped the back up herself. Then she let out another sigh.

"Gotta run."

"Where to?"

"Work," she spat out, staggering to her feet. I sat there on the edge of the bed watching her as she washed her face and passed a brush through her hair.

She kept her room neat but only to a degree, as if to make it any nicer wasn't worth the effort. Resignation hung heavily in the air.

The room was ten feet square and packed with cheap furniture, leaving enough space to lie down and no more. She stood there brushing her hair.

"What kind of work?"

"None of your business."

No argument there.

I kept silent for the interval it took a cigarette to burn itself out. She was peering in the mirror with her back to me, massaging the dark lines under her eyes with her fingertips.

"What time is it?" she asked again.

"Ten after nine."

"We've got to go. Put on your clothes and go home," she said, spraying her armpits with an aerosol can of eau de cologne. "You do have a home, don't you?"

"Yeah," I replied, pulling on my T-shirt as I sat there on the bed. I took a long last look out the window. "Where are you headed?"

"Near the harbor. What's it to you?"

"I'll give you a lift. That way you won't be late."

She stared at me, hairbrush in hand, looking as if she would burst into tears any minute. She'll feel better if she does, I thought. But she didn't.

"Look, let's get one thing clear. I drank too much, more than I could handle. Whatever happened after that is my responsibility."

She was slapping the handle of the brush against her hand in an almost businesslike manner. I didn't say anything, waiting for her to go on.

"Am I right?"

"Sure."

"But a guy who'll take advantage of a girl who's passed out . . . you can't get any lower than that."

"But we didn't do anything."

A moment passed. I could see her struggling to control her anger.

"Oh yeah? Then why was I naked?"

"You took your own clothes off."

"Fat chance!"

She hurled the brush on the bed and began hurriedly stuffing things into her shoulder bag. Wallet, lipstick, aspirin.

"Can you prove we didn't do anything?"

"Why don't you check and see?"

"How the hell could I do that?" She was seriously pissed off.

"You have my word of honor."

"I can't trust you."

"You have no choice." Now I was in a foul mood too.

Giving up on our conversation, she pushed me out of her room, followed me through the door, and locked it.

.   .   .

We walked along the asphalt path bordering the river to the vacant lot where my car was parked without so much as a single word.

I wiped the dust off the windshield with a tissue while she slowly circled the car, eyeing it with suspicion. She stopped to stare at the big white bull's head painted on the hood. The bull had a huge ring through his nose and a white rose between his teeth. He was smiling a lewd smile.

"Did you paint that?"

"No, the previous owner did."

"Why a bull?"

"Beats me."

She took two steps back to study the bull some more, then got in the car with her lips clamped shut, as if regretting having talked too much.

The car was stifling hot, but she smoked one cigarette after another in silence all the way to the harbor, mopping her sweat with a towel as she smoked. She would light one up, take three puffs, examine the lipstick stain on the filter, and then butt it out in the car's ashtray before firing up another.

"Hey, about last night. What did I say?" she exclaimed, when we reached our destination.

"All kinds of stuff."

"Like what? Tell me."

"Like about Kennedy, for example."

"Kennedy?"

"Yeah, John F. Kennedy."

She shook her head and sighed.

"I can't remember a thing."

. . .

When she got out of the car, she tucked a single thousand-yen bill behind my rearview mirror.

▸ **10**

It was a real scorcher of a night. Hot enough to soft-boil an egg.

The chill of the air-conditioning met me when I backed my way as usual through the heavy door of J's Bar, the stale aroma of cigarettes, whiskey, French fries, unwashed armpits, and bad plumbing all neatly layered like a Baumkuchen. I took my usual seat at the end of the bar, back against the wall, and surveyed the scene. There were three French sailors in an unfamiliar uniform, two girls they had brought with them, and a young couple who looked about twenty years old. That was it. No sign of the Rat.

I ordered a corned beef sandwich and a beer, pulled out my book, and leaned back to wait.

Ten minutes later, a thirtyish woman in a gaudy dress, with breasts like grapefruits, entered the bar and took a seat two down from mine. She scanned the room just as I had done and ordered a gimlet. When the drink came, she took one sip, got up, walked over to the pay phone, and made a call that seemed to go on forever. When the call was over, she grabbed her purse and disappeared into the toilet. This pattern repeated itself three times over the next forty minutes. Gimlet, long phone call, purse, toilet.

J the bartender came down to my end of the bar. "She'll wear her ass out at this rate," he muttered, a disgusted look on his face. J may be Chinese, but his Japanese is a hell of a lot better than mine.

When the woman came back from the toilet a third time, she glanced around the room and then slid into the seat beside me.

"I hate to ask," she said in a low voice, "but could you lend me some change?"

I dug the change out of my pocket and laid it on the counter. There were thirteen ten-yen coins in all.

"You're a doll. If I asked the bartender to break another bill, he'd just give me a dirty look."

"No problem. I feel a lot lighter now, thanks to you."

Smiling, she whisked the coins off the bar and disappeared in the direction of the phone.

So much for reading. I had J move the portable TV set to the counter and settled back with a beer to watch the baseball game. Some game, too. It was only the top of the fourth inning, but in that half inning two pitchers gave up six hits, including two home runs, and one outfielder collapsed from the strain. When the new pitcher was brought in, they ran six commercials: for beer, life insurance, vitamins, an airline, potato chips, and sanitary napkins.

The sailor, the one without a girl, I figured, came over to stand behind me, beer glass in hand.

"What are you watching?" he asked in French.

"Baseball," I replied in English.

"Beizeball?"

I gave him a simple breakdown of the rules. That guy throws the ball, that guy tries to whack it with his stick, and if he makes it all the way around the bases it counts as one run. The sailor watched for five minutes, but when a commercial began he asked why there were no Johnny Hallyday records on the jukebox.

"'Cause nobody likes him, that's why," I said.

"Then what French singers do people like here?"

"Adamo."

"He's Belgian."

"Okay, then Michel Polnareff."

"Merde," he swore, and headed back to his table.

It was the top of the fifth inning when the woman finally returned.

"Thanks," she said. "Let me buy you a drink in return."

"Don't sweat it."

"No, really. I'm a girl who likes to give back what she gets. For better or worse."

I tried to smile back but it didn't work, so I just nodded in reply. The woman summoned J with a raised finger and ordered a beer for me, another gimlet for herself. J gave three crisp nods and disappeared behind the end of the counter.

"Looks like I'm being stood up. You too?"

"Seems so."

"Is it a girl?"

"No, a guy."

"Then we're in the same boat. Gives us something to talk about."

I could only nod back.

"Tell me, how old do I look?"

"Twenty-eight."

"No, seriously."

"Okay, then twenty-six."

"What a bullshit artist! But you're nice," she said, laughing. "Do I look single? Or like I've got a husband?"

"Do I get a prize if I guess right?"

"Sure, why not."

"Okay, then I guess you're married."

"Mmm, you're half right. I got divorced last month. Ever talk to a divorcée before?"

"No, but I met a neuralgic cow once."

"Oh yeah? Where?"

"In the school lab. Took five of us to push it into the classroom."

The woman gave a hearty laugh.

"Then you go to college?"

"Yep."

"I was a college student once upon a time. Around 1960. Those were the good old days."

"How so?"

She chuckled to herself and took a sip of her gimlet. Then, as if suddenly remembering something, she looked at her wristwatch.

"Got to make another call," she said, standing up, purse in hand.

My unanswered question hovered in the air after she was gone.

I drank half the beer and asked J for my bill.

"Hightailing it, huh?" J said.

"Yeah."

"Not into older women, are you."

"It's got nothing to do with age. Give the Rat my best if he stops by."

When I left the bar, the woman was just embarking on her fourth visit to the toilet.

I found myself whistling in the car on the way home. It was a tune I had heard somewhere before, but I couldn't place it. A real oldie. I pulled over to the side of the road and sat there staring out at the ocean under the night sky, trying my best to remember.

Then I got it. It was "The Mickey Mouse Club Song."

Come along and sing a song and join the jamboree,
M-I-C, K-E-Y, M-O-U-S-E.

Maybe those really were the good old days.

▸ **11**

ON

Hey, all you out there. How're you feeling this evening? I'm feeling great myself, flying high, in fact. And I'm gonna try to bring you up to join me for the next two hours on your favorite program, *The Greatest Hits Request Show*, right here on NEB Radio. Yep, until nine o'clock on this beautiful Saturday night I'll be cranking out all those hot tunes you love to hear. Songs to warm your heart, songs to bring back memories, fun songs, songs to make you get up and dance. Songs you're sick of, songs that'll make you wanna puke—you name it, we play it. So keep those calls pouring in. You all know the number. Just remember: "Dial it wrong, you lose your song; dial it right, you cruise all night." Three syllables short of a haiku, but you can dig what I'm saying. Our lines opened at six, and for the last hour the phones have been ringing off the desks, all ten of them. You don't believe me? Here, get an earful of this . . . Far out, huh? Yessirree, we're cookin' now. Dial till your finger falls off. Got to apologize for last week, though. So many calls came in, we blew a fuse. But we're back in business now with a special cable they installed yesterday. Thing's as thick as an elephant's leg, let me tell you. "An elephant's calf, looks bigger by half, beside a giraffe." Darn, two syllables short this time! But you know where I'm coming from. Just lay back and let your fingers do the walking. Dial till you freak. Our staff here at the station may go nuts, but our fuse won't blow this time. Right? So here we go. Today was hot enough to bum anyone out, a real downer, so let's blow all those bad feelings away with the rock sounds you love to hear. After all, that's what great music is for, isn't it? Just like a dynamite chick. Okay, our first song of the evening. This one you can just sit back and enjoy. A great little number, and the best way to beat the heat. Brook Benton's "Rainy Night in Georgia."

> OFF

Whew . . . I'm boiling in here, no kidding . . . Hey, can't the air conditioner do any better than this? . . . It's hotter than hell . . . Give me a break, okay? I sweat like a pig, you know that . . .

Yeah, yeah, that's better . . .

Hey, I'm thirsty, can someone bring me a nice cold Coke? . . . No, don't worry, I won't have to take a leak. My bladder's like a steel drum . . . Blad-der, you've got it . . .

Thanks, Mi-chan. You're tops, babe . . . Aah, that bottle's nice and cold . . .

Hey, where's the freakin' opener? . . .

That's crazy. No way I can open this with my teeth . . . Quit horsing around—the record's ending. We haven't got time . . . Opener!

Shit!

ON

Brook Benton's "Rainy Night in Georgia." Great song. Feeling a bit cooler now? Guess how hot it got out there today, folks. Ninety-nine degrees! I don't care if it *is* summer, it's still too hot. A damn oven, is what it is. Ninety-nine means it's cooler to get it on with your girlfriend. Try to get your head around that one. Okay, I've talked enough. Let's spin another record. "Who'll Stop the Rain," by Creedence Clearwater Revival. Let's rock, baby!

OFF

. . . Hey, no sweat, I opened it with the corner of the mike stand . . .

. . . Whew, that hits the spot . . .

. . . Relax, I won't start hiccupping. You're kinda uptight, you know.

. . . What's the score of the baseball game? . . . It's on another station, right? . . .

. . . What? You've got to be kidding! This is a radio station, and we don't have a single radio? That's a criminal offense! . . .

. . . Okay, forget it. I'll take a beer instead. Make it nice and cold . . .

. . . Hey, I feel a hiccup coming on. Oh shit! . . .

. . . *Hic!* . . .

▸ **12**

The phone rang at 7:15. I was stretched out on my rattan chair in the living room, drinking a can of beer and popping cheese crackers into my mouth.

"A good evening to you, my friend. This is *The Greatest Hits Request Show* on NEB Radio. Are you listening to your radio?"

I took a hasty slug of beer to wash the remnants of the cheese crackers down my throat.

"Radio?"

"Yes, your radio. The greatest invention . . . *hic* . . . of modern civilization. More precise than a vacuum cleaner, smaller than a refrigerator, cheaper than a TV. And what are you doing right now, my friend?"

"Reading a book."

"That's a real no-no. You should be listening to your radio. Reading will just make you lonely. Catch my drift?"

"Uh-huh."

"A book is good for killing time when you're cooking spaghetti. Takes only one hand, get it?"

"Uh-huh."

"All right, then . . . *hic* . . . now we can talk. Ever hear a DJ with hiccups before?"

"No."

"Then it's the first time. Same as for all you listeners out there. So do you know why we're calling you now, in the middle of our broadcast?"

"No."

"Because, my friend, it just so happens . . . *hic* . . . a young lady has asked us to dedicate a song to you. Can you guess who she is?"

"No."

"She has requested that blast from the past, 'California Girls,' by the Beach Boys. Ring a bell?"

I thought for a moment, but nothing popped into my head.

"C'mon now, you've got to do better than that. Guess right and you'll receive a special T-shirt in the mail."

I thought again. This time I could feel an infinitesimal something tugging at a corner of my memory.

" 'California Girls' . . . the Beach Boys . . . any luck?"

"Come to think of it, about five years ago a girl in my high school class lent me that record."

"What kind of girl?"

"I helped her find her contact lens on one of our school trips. So she thanked me by lending me the record."

"Contact lens, huh? . . . So did you return the record?"

"No, I lost it somewhere."

"Big mistake. You should have bought her a new copy. With

women it's okay if they owe you . . . *hic* . . . but not if you owe them. Got it?"

"Yes."

"All right then. So that girl whose contact lens you found on a school trip five years ago is listening in right now, aren't you, baby? Can you give me her name?"

Finally, the name popped into my head. I told him.

"So there you go, young lady. It looks as if he's finally going to return that record. Made your day, I bet . . . By the way, how old are you?"

"Twenty-one."

"Great age. Student?"

"Yes."

". . . *hic* . . ."

"Huh?"

"And what are you majoring in?"

"Biology."

"So you're into animals?"

"Uh-huh."

"What is it about them that you like?"

"Maybe it's because they don't laugh."

"Ah, animals don't laugh?"

"Well, dogs and horses do a little."

"Like when?"

"When they're happy."

I could feel myself getting mad for the first time in years.

"So then . . . *hic* . . . a dog could be a stand-up comic, couldn't he."

"You're proof of that."

"Hahahahaha."

▸ **13**

Well, East Coast girls are hip,
I really dig those styles they wear,
And the Southern girls with the way they talk
They knock me out when I'm down there.

The Midwest farmers' daughters
Really make you feel alright,
And the Northern girls with the way they kiss,
They keep their boyfriends warm at night.

I wish they all could be California girls . . .

▸ **14**

The T-shirt arrived in the afternoon mail three days later.
It looked like this.

▶ **15**

The following morning, I put on the scratchy new T-shirt and strolled the streets of the harbor town. Spotting a small record shop, I pushed open the door and went in. No other customers were there, just a very bored-looking young woman at the counter sipping a can of Coke as she checked sales slips. It took several minutes of shuffling through the record shelves before I realized I had seen her before. She was the girl with no little finger, the one I had found passed out on the bathroom floor a week earlier. "Hey," I said. Startled, she looked at me, then at my T-shirt, then drained the rest of her Coke.

"How'd you find out where I worked?" she asked in a voice steeped in resignation.

"Pure chance. I came to buy records."

"What're you looking for?"

"The Beach Boys LP with the song 'California Girls.'"

She nodded a skeptical nod, got up, strode over to the shelves, grabbed a record, and brought it back like a well-trained dog.

"This is it, right?"

I nodded. With my hands still jammed in my pockets, I scanned the store.

"I'd also like Beethoven's Piano Concerto number 3."

This time she came back carrying two records.

"We've got Glenn Gould and Backhaus. Which do you want?"

"Glenn Gould."

She put one record on the counter and returned the other to the shelf.

"Anything else?"

"The Miles Davis album that has 'A Gal in Calico.' "

This took a little extra time, but she came back with the record.

"Next?"

"That's it. Thanks."

"Are these all for you?" she asked, lining up the three records on the counter.

"No. They're presents."

"A bighearted guy, huh?"

"So it would seem."

She shrugged uncomfortably and added up the bill: 5550 yen. I paid and took the parcel.

"Well, anyway, thanks to you I was able to sell three records before noon."

"My pleasure."

She sat back down behind the counter with a sigh and resumed going through the sales slips.

"So are you always here by yourself?"

"Another girl works with me. She's at lunch right now."

"And you?"

"I'll go eat when she comes back."

I pulled out my cigarettes, lit one, and stood there watching her work.

"Hey," I said. "How about we have lunch together?"

She shook her head. "I like eating alone," she said, her eyes never leaving the slips.

"I'm the same way."

"Really?" She set the sales slips down with a weary sigh, put the new Harpers Bizarre album on the turntable, and lowered the needle. "Then why do you ask?"

"I try to change things up every once in a while."

"Change by yourself." She pulled the stack of slips closer and went back to work. "Now please leave me alone."

I nodded.

"I told you this once before, but I think you're scum." Pursing her lips, she went back to flipping through the slips with her four fingers.

▸ **16**

When I entered J's Bar, the Rat was already there, his elbows propped on the counter and a frown on his face, plowing through a Henry James novel as thick as a telephone directory.

"Is that any good?" I asked.

The Rat raised his face from the book and shook his head no. "Still," he said, "I've been reading a lot. Since the last time I saw you. Know who said, 'I love a magnificent falsehood more than an impoverished truth'?"

"Nope."

"Roger Vadim. French director. How about, 'The test of a first-rate intelligence is its ability to function while holding two opposite ideas at the same time'?"

"Who said that?"

"I forget. But do you buy it?"

"I think it's bull."

"How come?"

"Let's say you wake up starving at 3 a.m. You check the fridge but it's empty. So what do you do?"

The Rat pondered this for a moment, then burst out laughing.

I called J over and ordered a beer and some fries, pulled out a package containing one of the records, and handed it to the Rat.

"What the hell is this?"

"Your birthday present."

"That's not till next month."

"I'll be gone by then."

The Rat sat there thinking, the unopened package in his hand.

"Yeah, it's going to be lonely without you around," he said, taking out the record and looking at it. "Beethoven's Piano Concerto number 3, Glenn Gould, Leonard Bernstein. Mmm. Haven't heard it. Have you?"

"Nope."

"All the same, I really like this! To be blunt."

▸ **17**

I tried to track down her phone number for three days. The number of the girl who lent me the Beach Boys record, that is.

The first day, I visited the office of our old high school and found a listing for her in the registry of graduates. When I called, though, all I got was a recording saying that the number was no longer in service. I dialed information and gave the operator her name, but after searching for five minutes she came back on the line to announce that no party by that name was listed in the directory. I liked the ring of "no party by that name." I thanked her and hung up.

The second day, I began phoning other members of our class to see if they knew where she was, but not only did none of them know anything, most had forgotten she even existed. For some unknown reason, the last person I called snapped, "I don't have time to talk to a shit like you," and slammed down the phone.

The third day, I went back to our high school office and asked them to look up the name of the college she'd attended after graduation. It turned out she had enrolled in the English department of a second-rate school in central Tokyo. I phoned their office and told them that I ran the information desk at the McCormack Salad Dressing Corporation, and that I needed to find out her correct name and address to contact her about a survey we were doing. I hated to bother them, I added politely, but it was, after all, a very important matter. The guy said he would look, and asked me to call back again in fifteen minutes. I had a beer while I waited, but when I called back he told me that she had officially withdrawn from school in March. The reason, he said, was to recuperate from illness, but he had no knowledge of what the illness was, whether she had recovered to the point she could eat salad, or why she had chosen to drop out instead of taking a leave of absence.

Even an old address might help, I told him, so he checked their records for me. The number he gave me was that of a boardinghouse not far from the college. When I phoned, a person who sounded like the landlady answered: the girl had left in the spring for goodness knows where, she said, and then hung up. The way the line went dead made it clear she didn't want to know, either.

That severed the last link between the girl and me.

I went home, opened a beer, and sat back to listen to "California Girls" by myself.

▸ **18**

The phone rang. I was half asleep on my wicker chair, gazing with bleary eyes at the open book in my lap. An evening shower had come and gone, leaving the trees in the garden dripping. Then came a south wind that smelled of the ocean. It shook the leaves of the potted plants on the balcony and ruffled the curtains.

"Hello," said a woman. She spoke like someone trying to balance a very fragile glass on a very wobbly table. "Remember me?"

I pretended to be trying to place her for a moment.

"How's the record business?" I asked.

"Not so hot. Business is bad all over, I guess. People just aren't into records."

"Oh yeah?"

I could hear her tapping her nails against the receiver.

"I had a hard time finding your number."

"Oh yeah?"

"I had to go to J's Bar. The guy who works there asked your friend for me. You know, tall guy, kind of weird. He was reading Molière."

"No kidding."

Silence.

"Everyone's wondering where you disappeared to the past week. They're all worried you're sick or something."

"I didn't realize I was so popular."

She paused. "Are you angry with me?"

"Why do you ask?"

"I said some really mean things. I just wanted to apologize."

"Look, I don't need your sympathy. If it's bothering you, go to the park and feed the pigeons."

She sighed. I could hear her lighting up a cigarette at the other end of the line. Then came the sound of Bob Dylan's *Nashville Skyline*. She was probably phoning from work.

"Your feelings aren't the problem. I just shouldn't have spoken to you like that." She was talking very quickly.

"You're pretty hard on yourself."

"Yes, I try to be."

She was quiet for a moment.

"Any chance I could see you tonight?" she said finally.

"Sure."

"Eight o'clock at J's?"

"Got it."

Another pause. "Listen, I've had a rough time recently."

"I understand."

"Thanks."

She hung up.

▸ **19**

To keep it short and sweet: I'm twenty-one years old. Still plenty young, but not as young as I used to be. If that bothered me, my only option would be to take a flying leap off the Empire State Building some Sunday morning.

Here's a joke I heard in an old movie about the Great Depression: "Every time I pass the Empire State Building, I open my umbrella. I mean, it's raining people there."

So, like I said, I'm twenty-one. No plans to die yet. I've slept with three girls so far.

The first was a high school classmate. We were both seventeen, and we believed it was true love. We found a spot in the bushes one evening; then she removed her brown loafers, her white wool socks, her pale green seersucker dress, her odd underwear (I could tell right away they didn't fit), and last of all, after a moment's hesitation, her wristwatch. Then we made love on the Sunday edition of the *Asahi* newspaper.

We broke up all of a sudden just a few months after graduation. I can't remember why now—the reason was that trivial. Haven't laid eyes on her since then, either. I think of her sometimes at night when I can't fall asleep. End of story.

The second girl I slept with was a hippie chick I bumped into in the Shinjuku subway station. She had nowhere to stay and was flat broke (her chest was pretty flat too), but she had beautiful, intelligent eyes. The most violent antiwar demonstration Shinjuku had ever seen was raging that night, and the trains, buses, and everything else were completely shut down.

"If you hang around here you're going to get busted," I told her. She was squatting inside the chained subway entrance reading a sports newspaper that she'd plucked from the garbage.

"At least they'll feed me."

"It won't be pretty."

"I'm used to it."

I lit a cigarette and gave one to her. My eyes were smarting from all the tear gas.

"Have you eaten anything today?"

"Not since this morning."

"Let me buy you something. We can't hang around here any longer."

"Why would you want to treat me?"

I didn't know the answer to that one myself, but I dragged

her out of the subway, and we walked down the deserted streets all the way to Mejiro.

For the next week, this quiet girl crashed in my apartment. She would wake up after noon, eat, smoke, dawdle over a book, watch some TV, and sometimes have half-hearted sex with me. Her only possession was a white canvas bag that held a thick windbreaker, two T-shirts, a pair of jeans, three soiled pairs of underwear, and a box of tampons.

"Where are you from?" I asked her once.

"No place you've ever heard of," she answered, and clammed up.

When I came back from the supermarket one day carrying a bag of groceries, she had vanished. Her white bag had vanished too. Not to mention a number of other things. Like the few coins I had left scattered on my desk, a carton of cigarettes, and my freshly laundered T-shirt. A sheet torn from one of my writing pads sat on the desk, an apparent farewell note. It consisted of a single word—"Asshole." I guess she meant me.

The third girl I slept with was a French literature major I met in the school library, but the following spring vacation she hanged herself in the shabby grove of trees by the tennis courts. Her body wasn't discovered until vacation ended and the new school year began—she had been swinging in the wind for two whole weeks. Even today no one goes near that grove after the sun goes down.

▶ **20**

She was sitting at the counter of J's Bar, looking uncomfortable and stirring what little was left of the ice in her glass of ginger ale with a straw.

"I thought you weren't coming," she said, sounding a bit relieved.

"I don't stand people up. I just had something to do before I left."

"What kind of something?"

"Shoes. I was polishing a pair of shoes."

"Those sneakers?" she said in a skeptical voice, pointing at my basketball shoes.

"Fat chance. No, my father's shoes. It's one of the rules of our house. He believes that children should polish their father's shoes."

"Why?"

"Beats me. I guess he sees it as a symbol of something. At any rate, he comes home every night at eight, like clockwork. So before then, I polish his shoes and then run off to grab a beer."

"That's a nice habit."

"You really think so?"

"Yeah. You should be grateful."

"I'm grateful he only has two feet."

She giggled.

"You must come from a respectable family."

"Yeah, right. Respectable *and* broke. Makes me so happy I could cry."

"But," she said, still stirring her watery ginger ale with the tip of her straw, "my family was a lot poorer."

."How can you tell?"

"By smell. Just like the rich can smell the rich, the poor can sniff out who's poor."

I poured the beer J had given me into my glass.

"So where are your parents these days?"

"I don't feel like talking about it."

"How come?"

"Respectable people don't talk to strangers about family problems. Isn't that so?"

"Are you a respectable person?"

She pondered this for a full fifteen seconds.

"I'm hoping to be. Trying my best, anyway. Isn't everyone like that?"

I chose not to answer.

"Still, you should talk about that stuff," I said.

"Why?"

"For one thing, you'll have to tell someone at some point anyway; for another, if you tell me, I'll keep my mouth shut."

She smiled, lit a cigarette, and took three drags on it while she studied the grain of the wood-paneled bar.

"Five years ago," she began, breaking the silence, "my father died of brain cancer. It was awful. He suffered for two whole years. All the money we had in the world was spent on his illness. It left us flat broke. Then, to make things even worse, the family fell apart. We were just too worn out. Those things happen, right?"

I nodded. "So, what happened to your mother?"

"She's living somewhere. She sends me New Year's cards."

"Sounds as if you don't like her very much."

"Yeah."

"Any brothers or sisters?"

"I have a twin sister. That's all."

"Where's she?"

"Thirty thousand light-years away."

She gave a nervous laugh and pushed her ginger ale to the side.

"It's never a good idea to bad-mouth your family," she continued. "Only leaves you down in the dumps."

"Don't let it get to you. Everybody's carrying stuff like that around."

"You too?"

"Yeah, every morning I clutch my can of shaving cream and weep."

She laughed happily. It sounded as if she hadn't laughed in years.

"So how come you're drinking ginger ale?" I asked. "I can't see you being on the wagon."

"Mm, that was the idea. But I'll have a drink now."

"So what'll it be?"

"White wine, the colder the better."

I called J over and ordered a glass of wine for her and another beer for me.

"So what's it like having a twin sister?"

"It feels kind of weird. I mean, you've got the same face, the same IQ, the same bra size . . . it's a real turnoff."

"Did people confuse the two of you a lot?"

"Until we were eight they did. Once I was down to nine fingers, though, they didn't make that mistake anymore."

She placed both hands on the bar, neatly lining her fingers up like a concert pianist preparing to play. I took her left hand in mine and examined it closely under the recessed lights. It was small and as cool as a cocktail glass, the three fingers and thumb complete and natural, as if they'd been that way from birth. Indeed, their naturalness seemed almost miraculous, a lot more convincing than six fingers would have been anyway.

"I got my little finger caught in a vacuum cleaner when I was eight. It popped off just like that."

"Where is it now?"

"Where is what now?"

"Your little finger."

"I forget," she said, laughing. "You know, you're the first person to ever ask that."

"Does it bother you to be missing your little finger?"

"It does when I'm wearing gloves."

"Any other times?"

She shook her head. "I'd be lying if I said never. But it's no worse than girls who worry about fat necks or hairy legs."

I nodded.

"So what do you do?" she asked.

"I go to college. In Tokyo."

"Home for vacation."

"Yeah, you got it."

"What are you studying?"

"Biology. I love animals."

"Me too."

I drained my glass of beer and grabbed a handful of fries.

"Hey . . . there was a famous leopard in Bhagalpur that killed and ate three hundred and fifty Indians in just three years."

"Really?"

"An Englishman, Colonel Jim Corbett, who was known as

the leopard exterminator, shot one hundred and twenty-five tigers and leopards, including that one, in eight years. So do you still love animals?"

She stubbed out her smoke, took a sip of wine, and studied my face for a moment. "You know," she said, looking impressed, "you really are a little nuts."

▶ **21**

Half a month after my third girlfriend killed herself, I was reading Jules Michelet's *La Sorcière*. A great book. Anyway, I came across this passage:

> In the work he dedicated to the Cardinal of Lorraine in 1596, the prosecutor M. Remy owns to having burnt eight hundred witches, in sixteen years. "So well do I deal out judgements," he says, "that last year sixteen slew themselves to avoid passing through my hands." (tr. Lionel James Trottier, 1863)

For some reason, I find the phrase "So well do I deal out judgements" cool in the extreme.

▶ **22**

The telephone rang. I was in the midst of applying calamine lotion to my face, which was sunburned from my daily trips to the local pool. After ten rings, I gave up, peeled off the neat checkerboard of cotton squares, and rose from my chair to answer it.

"Hey there. It's me."

"Ah, so it's you."

"Whatcha doing?"

"Nothing much."

I patted my stinging face with the towel that was wrapped around my neck.

"I enjoyed myself last night. First time in a long while."

"Glad to hear it."

"So . . . do you like beef stew?"

"Uh-huh."

"I just made a whole pot. More than I could put away in a week. Want to come over and help me eat it?"

"Sounds good."

"Okay. Come in an hour. If you're not here by then, I'll chuck it all in the garbage. Got it?"

"But . . ."

"I hate waiting. See ya."

She hung up before I could open my mouth.

I lay on the sofa for the next ten minutes, staring at the ceiling and listening to the Top 40 on the radio. Then I took a shower, shaved myself smooth and clean under the hot water, and put on a pair of Bermuda shorts, and a shirt just back from the cleaners. It was a pleasant evening. I watched the sun set as I drove along the coastal road, stopping to buy two bottles of chilled white wine and a carton of cigarettes before getting on the highway.

.　　.　　.

She cleared the table and laid out white plates and bowls, while I pried the cork from a bottle of wine with a fruit knife. The room was steaming from the bubbling stew.

"I didn't know it would get this hot," she said. "It's hot as hell."

"Hell is hotter."

"Sounds like you've been there."

"I heard it from someone. They make it hotter and hotter till you think you'll go crazy; then they move you someplace cooler for a while. Then when you've recovered a little they move you back again."

"So hell is like a sauna."

"Yeah, more or less. But a few can't recover and go totally bonkers."

"So what happens to them?"

"They get sent up to heaven, where they're forced to paint the walls. You see, the walls in heaven have to be kept a perfect white. The slightest smudge is unacceptable. It's an image thing. As a result, they have to keep painting from dawn till dusk every day. It messes up their respiratory systems big time."

She stopped asking questions after that. I carefully scooped out the bits of cork that had fallen into the bottle and poured us each a glass.

"To cold wine and warm hearts," she toasted me.

"Say what?"

"It's from a TV commercial. Cold wine and warm hearts. You haven't seen it?"

"Nope."

"Don't you watch TV?"

"Once in a while. I used to watch a lot. My favorite was *Lassie*. The one with the original dog, that is."

"That's right, you love animals."

"Uh-huh."

"I can watch all day long when I've got the time. You name it, I watch it. Yesterday, I saw a debate between a biologist and a chemist. Did you catch that one?"

"No."

She took a swallow of wine and gave a small shake of her head, as if remembering the moment.

"You know, Pascal had what they call scientific intuition."

"Scientific intuition?"

"Like, an ordinary scientist thinks: A equals B, B equals C, therefore A equals C. QED. Right?"

I nodded.

"But Pascal's mind worked in a different way. He just thought, A equals C. He wasn't interested in proof. But time confirmed his theories, and he came up with all kinds of valuable discoveries."

"Like vaccines."

She put her wine down and looked at me, appalled.

"Vaccines? Wasn't that Jenner? How'd you pass the college entrance exams, anyway?"

"Then, maybe antibodies for rabies, and low-temperature sterilization?"

"Ding-dong."

She gave a self-satisfied smirk, drained her glass, and refilled it herself.

"In the TV debate, they called that ability 'scientific intuition.' Think you might have it?"

"Hardly."

"Think you'd like some?"

"It might come in handy. Like when I'm in bed with a girl."

She laughed and headed off to the kitchen, returning with a pot of stew, a bowl of salad, and some rolls. At last a cool breeze reached us through the wide-open windows.

We sat back and ate a relaxed dinner while listening to her records. She asked me lots of questions, mostly about my school and my life in Tokyo. Pretty boring stuff. I told her about the cat experiments we carried out. (Of course, I lied that we never killed them. That we were just testing their brain functions. In fact, over the course of a mere two months, I was solely responsible for snuffing out the lives of thirty-six cats of all sizes and shapes.) I told her about the demonstrations and the student strikes. I showed her where a riot cop had knocked out one of my front teeth.

"Don't you want to get even?"

"Are you kidding?"

"Why not? If it were me, I'd track down that cop and knock out a whole bunch of his teeth with a hammer."

"Well, I'm me, and as far as I'm concerned it's over and done with. I wouldn't know who to go after anyway—all those riot cops look the same."

"So then there's no meaning, right?"

"Meaning?"

"No meaning to having your tooth knocked out."

"Nope."

She let out a weary groan and took another bite of stew.

.   .   .

After dinner, we drank a cup of coffee, washed the dishes side by side in the tiny kitchen, went back to the table, lit a cigarette, and listened to the MJQ on her record player.

I could see her nipples clearly through her thin blouse, and her cotton shorts were loose around her hips. To make matters even worse, our legs kept colliding under the table. My face grew redder each time they touched.

"Was dinner good?"

"It was delicious."

"Then why didn't you say so sooner?" she said, biting her lower lip.

"It's a bad habit. I always forget the important stuff."

"Can I let you in on something?"

"Sure."

"If you don't change that habit you're gonna be the loser."

"I know. But I'm like an old jalopy. Fix one thing and another breaks down."

She laughed and put Marvin Gaye on the turntable. The clock said almost eight.

"No shoes to be shined today?"

"I do that before I go to bed. When I brush my teeth."

She was peering into my eyes as she talked, her slender elbows propped on the table, her chin cupped in her hands. Her gaze was starting to get to me. I tried to escape it by lighting up cigarettes and pretending to look out the window, but that only added to her amusement.

"So I guess I can believe you," she said.

"Believe what?"

"That you didn't mess with me the other night."

"How so?"

"You really want me to tell you?"

"No."

"I knew you'd say that," she said, giggling. She filled my glass, then looked out the darkened window, as if considering something. "Sometimes, I imagine how great it would be if we could live our lives without bothering other people. Think it's possible?"

"I wonder."

"So tell me, am I bothering you?"

"I'm okay."

"So far, you mean."

"Yeah, so far."

She reached across the table and laid her hand on mine, left it there for a moment, then withdrew it.

"I'm taking a trip tomorrow," she said.

"A trip to where?"

"Haven't decided yet. Some place quiet and cool, that's the plan anyway. For about a week."

I nodded.

"I'll call you when I get back."

*

In the car on my way home, I suddenly remembered my first date. Seven years before.

Now, it feels like I never stopped asking the girl, "Sure you're not bored?"

We had gone to see an Elvis Presley movie. The lyrics of the theme song went like this:

We had a quarrel, a lovers' spat,
I write I'm sorry but the letter keeps coming back.
She wrote upon it:
Return to Sender, Address Unknown,
No Such Number, No Such Zone.

Time goes by so damn fast.

▸ **23**

The third girl I slept with liked to call my penis my *"raison d'être."*

*

A while before that, I had tried writing a short story whose theme was the meaning of life. I never finished it, but the process of thinking about people's *raison d'être* produced a strange frame of mind, a kind of obsession, in fact, that compelled me to convert everything in my life into numbers. This condition lasted for about eight months, during which I had to count the number of people in the car the moment I boarded a train, the number of steps of each staircase I climbed, even my own pulse if I had the time. According to my records, from August 15, 1969, until April 3rd of the following year, I attended 358 lectures, had sex 54 times, and smoked 6,921 cigarettes.

I believed in all seriousness that by converting my life into numbers I might be able to get through to people. That having something to communicate could stand as proof I really existed.

Of course, no one had the slightest interest in how many cigarettes I had smoked, or the number of stairs I had climbed, or
the size of my penis. When I realized this, I lost my *raison d'être*
and became utterly alone.

*

And so, when the news of her death reached me, I was smoking
my 6,922nd cigarette.

> ▶ **24**

The Rat didn't touch a drop of beer that night. Not a good sign,
for sure. Instead he knocked off five Jim Beams on the rocks in
quick succession.

We were in the dim innermost corner of J's Bar, killing time
at the pinball machine, that piece of junk that offers dead time
in return for small change. The Rat, though, was the kind of
guy who took everything seriously. So it was almost a miracle
that I beat him in two of the six games we played.

"What's with you tonight, anyway?"

"Nothing," the Rat answered.

Back we went to the bar for more beer and Jim Beam.

We sat there in sullen silence, listening to one song after
another on the jukebox: "Everyday People," "Woodstock,"
"Spirit in the Sky," "Hey There Lonely Girl."

"Got a favor to ask," the Rat said.

"What kind?"

"I want you to meet someone."

"A girl?"

The Rat hesitated before nodding yes.

"Why ask me?"

"Anyone else around?" the Rat shot back, launching into his sixth Jim Beam. "Oh yeah, do you own a suit and tie?"

"Sure. Still . . ."

"Then it's tomorrow at two," the Rat said. "Hey, what do girls eat to stay alive, anyway?"

"Shoe soles."

"Get out of here," the Rat said.

▸ **25**

The Rat's favorite food was pancakes, hot off the griddle. He would stack several in a deep dish, cut them into four neat pieces, then pour a bottle of Coke over the top.

The first time I visited the Rat's home, he had pulled a table out into the balmy May sunlight and was hard at work shoveling this concoction into his mouth.

"This meal's outstanding feature," he said, "is the perfect way it blends solid food and drink."

Wild birds of every shape and hue had gathered in the big wooded yard and were intently pecking at the white popcorn strewn across the lawn.

▸ **26**

Now I'm going to tell you about the third girl I ever slept with.

It's hard enough to talk about the dead under normal circumstances, but it's even harder to talk about girls who have died young: by dying, they stay young forever.

We, on the other hand, advance in age every year, every month, every day. There are times when I can even feel myself aging by the hour. The scary thing is, it's true.

*

She was no beauty. Yet to say "no beauty" may not be fair. It would be more proper to say, "Her beauty did not reach the level that did her justice."

I have just one photograph of her. Someone jotted the date on the back—August 1963. The same year Kennedy took a bullet in the head. It seems to have been snapped at a summer resort, and shows her perched on a sea wall smiling a somewhat uncomfortable smile. Her hair is clipped short à la Jean Seberg (a style I somehow connected with Auschwitz then), and she is wearing a long red gingham dress. She looks a bit awkward, and lovely. It is a loveliness that touches the heart.

Her lips are slightly parted, her nose is pert, like a delicate antenna, the bangs she seems to have cut herself fall artlessly over a broad forehead, and there are the faint remnants of pimples on her full cheeks.

She was fourteen then, and it was the most beautiful moment in her twenty-one years on this planet. Then, suddenly, that moment vanished. That's all I know. I have no way of understanding why, or what possible purpose it may have served. No one does.

*

She said, in all seriousness—no joke—that she had come to college in order to receive a divine revelation. She told me this a little before four in the morning, when we were lying naked in bed. I asked her what a divine revelation was like.

"How the heck would I know," she said. A minute later she added, "But whatever it is, it flies down from heaven like a pair of angel wings."

I imagined a pair of angel wings descending on the central square of our school. Viewed from a distance, they looked like tissue paper.

*

No one knows why she chose to die. I doubt somehow that she did either.

▸ **27**

I had an unpleasant dream. I was a big black bird flying westward over a thick jungle. I was badly wounded, my feathers caked with black blood. Ominous dark clouds were gathering in the western sky, and there was a whiff of rain in the air.

I hadn't dreamed for a long time. So long, in fact, that it took a while to realize what had just happened.

I got out of bed, showered off the nasty sweat, and had a breakfast of toast and apple juice. Beer and cigarettes had left my throat feeling stuffed with old cotton. I chucked the dirty dishes into the sink and selected an olive-green cotton suit, the most neatly pressed shirt I could find, and a black knit tie. I carried them out to the front room and sat down beside the air conditioner.

The TV news was predicting, in triumphant tones, that this might be the hottest day of the summer. I switched off the set and went into my older brother's room next door, chose a few books from the massive pile, took them to the front room, and stretched out on the couch.

Two years earlier, my brother had taken off for America without a word of explanation, leaving behind a roomful of books and a girlfriend. She and I still got together for a meal every so often. According to her, my brother and I were very similar. This came as something of a shock.

"Like where exactly?" I asked.

"Like everywhere," she said.

Maybe she was right. After all, we'd been taking turns shining the same shoes for more than ten years.

When twelve o'clock rolled around, I fastened my tie, put on my jacket, and headed out the door, already fed up with the heat awaiting me.

I had time to kill, so I decided to cruise around. Our town occupied a pitifully long and narrow strip running from the ocean up to the foot of the mountains. It never changed: a river and a tennis court, a golf course, a lengthy row of large houses, walls upon walls, a handful of tidy restaurants and boutiques, an old library, fields filled with evening primrose, a park with a monkey cage.

I drove the streets that snaked through the hilly residential area before taking the river road down almost to the ocean, where I stopped to cool my feet in the fresh water. Two girls wearing white hats, sunglasses, and deep tans were batting a ball back and forth on the tennis court nearby. The midday sun was scorching, and each swing of their rackets sent a spray of sweat flying across the court.

I watched them for five minutes, then returned to the car, put the seat back, closed my eyes, and listened to the whack of balls mingled with the sound of the surf. The whiff of ocean on the southern breeze and the smell of burning asphalt carried with them memories of summers past. It had seemed as though those sweet dreams of summer would last forever: the warmth of a girl's skin, an old rock 'n' roll song, a freshly washed button-down shirt, the odor of cigarette smoke in a pool changing room, a fleeting premonition. Then one summer (when had it been?) the dreams had vanished, never to return.

When I drove up to J's Bar at 2 p.m. on the dot, the Rat was sitting on the guardrail engrossed in a copy of Kazantzakis's *The Last Temptation of Christ*. "So where is she?" I asked.

The Rat closed the book and slipped into the seat beside me. He put his sunglasses on. "It's a no go," he said.

"No go?"

"Yeah, I gave it up."

I sighed, loosened my tie, tossed my jacket in the backseat, and lit up a smoke.

"So where are we headed?"

"The zoo."

"Sounds good to me," I said.

▸ **28**

Now I'll talk about the town. I was born and raised in it, and it was there that I slept with my first girl.

The ocean is in front of the town, with mountains to the rear and a giant port next door. It is a tiny place. I quit trying to light up on my way home from the port because by the time I struck the match I had missed the highway turnoff.

The population is slightly over seventy thousand, a number that's not likely to change in the next five years. Most families live in two-story homes with attached gardens, and they own one car, though quite a few have two.

I didn't pluck these figures out of the air—rather, they are officially announced at the close of each year by the statistics office at city hall. Their attentiveness to the number of two-story homes is a nice touch.

The Rat's home had three stories topped off by a glassed-in roof garden. The Rat's father's Mercedes-Benz and the Rat's Triumph TR3 sat grill to grill in a basement garage carved into the slope. Strangely, the garage had the most homey feel of the entire place. It was big enough to accommodate a Piper Cub and was packed with old televisions and refrigerators, a sofa and coffee table set, stereo equipment, sideboards, and anything else that had been replaced by newer, more up-to-date models. The Rat and I spent many pleasant hours there drinking beer.

I knew almost nothing about the Rat's father. We never met.

When I asked the Rat what he was like, all I got was the flat statement "Someone a whole lot older than me—also male."

Rumor had it that the Rat's father had been penniless before the war. On the eve of hostilities, though, he had managed, after much difficulty, to lay his hands on a small chemical factory, where he began producing insect repellent cream. There was considerable doubt as to its effectiveness, but, fortunately for him, the war spread to the South Pacific at that juncture, and the stuff flew off the shelves.

When the war ended, the Rat's father moved his stock of ointment into warehouses and began marketing a sketchy health tonic; then, toward the end of the Korean War, in an abrupt move, he shifted to household cleaners. Rumor has it that the ingredients were identical in all cases. Not inconceivable.

In other words, the same ointment slathered on the heaped bodies of Japanese soldiers in the jungles of New Guinea twenty-five years ago can today be found, with the same trademark, gracing the toilets of the nation as a drain cleaner.

Thus did the Rat's father join the ranks of the wealthy.

Of course, I had poor friends too. One of them had a father who drove a city bus. Now, there may be rich bus drivers, but my friend's father was one of the poor ones. I hung out at his house a lot since his parents were rarely there. His father would either be driving his bus or at the racetrack, while his mother worked part-time jobs all day long.

He and I were in the same high school class, and one particular incident made us friends.

I was taking a leak during our lunch break one day when he

slipped into the next spot and pulled down his fly. We didn't talk, but we finished up at the same time and washed our hands together.

"Hey, I've got something here that'll knock your socks off," he said, wiping his hands on the seat of his pants.

"Oh yeah?"

"Wanna see?"

He pulled a photograph from his wallet and passed it to me. It showed a woman with her legs spread wide plunging a beer bottle into herself.

"Pretty wild, huh?"

"No kidding."

"I've got even better stuff at home if you want to come over."

And so it was that the two of us became friends.

The town was home to many kinds of people. In the eighteen years I lived there I learned a great deal. My emotional roots are there, and almost all my memories are connected to the place. Nevertheless, the spring I entered university, I heaved a deep sigh of relief when I left.

I still come back for spring and summer vacation, but basically all I do is drink beer.

▶ **29**

The Rat had been in the pits for about a week. The approach of autumn probably had something to do with it, and perhaps the girl he had asked me to meet did too. The Rat didn't have anything to say on the subject.

I tried prying some information out of J when the Rat wasn't around.

"What do you think has got the Rat down?" I asked him.

"I can't figure it out either," he said. "Maybe it's because summer's ending."

The Rat's mood darkened as autumn approached. He sat at the counter glancing at some book or other, and if I tried to talk to him, all I got in response was a half-assed crack of some kind. When the evening breezes turned cool and the first whiff of autumn rose in the air, he gave up beer for a steady diet of bourbon on the rocks, shoveling coins into the jukebox beside the counter and kicking the pinball machine around until the Tilt sign flashed, much to J's alarm.

"I guess he feels he's being left behind," J said. "I can see why."

"How so?"

"Everybody's heading off someplace. Back to college or back to work. You too, right?"

"I see what you mean."

"Think how he feels."

I nodded. "And the girl?"

"Believe me, he'll forget her before long."

"Did something bad happen?"

"You got me," J said, and went back to his work. Swallowing my questions, I went over to the jukebox, chose a few tunes, and returned to the bar and my beer.

J came back about ten minutes later.

"Hey," he said. "Didn't the Rat tell you anything?"

"Nope."

"That's strange."

"Really?"

J stood there for a minute, polishing the glass in his hand.

"I bet he wants to talk to you about whatever it is."

"Then why doesn't he?"

"He's afraid. That you'll make fun of him."

"I would never do that."

"Still, it looks like that sometimes. That's how I've always seen it, anyway. You're a sweet kid, but part of you seems—how should I put this?—above it all, like a Zen monk or something . . . It's not really a criticism."

"No offense taken."

"But, you know, I'm twenty years older, and I've been through a lot more. So I get sort of . . ."

"Old-womanish."

"Yeah."

I smiled and took another swig of beer.

"I'll talk to the Rat."

"Good idea."

J stubbed out his smoke and went back to work, and I made a trip to the john. While washing up, I peeked at my face in the mirror. That bummed me out so much I had another beer.

▸ **30**

There was a time when everyone wanted to be cool.

Toward the end of high school, I decided to express only half of what I was really feeling. I can't recall the initial reason, but for the next several years this was how I behaved. At which point I discovered that I had turned into a person incapable of expressing more than half of what he felt.

I don't know what that has to do with being cool. But if a fridge that has to be defrosted all year round can be called cool, then that's what I was.

And so I continue writing this, plying my consciousness with cigarettes and beer to prevent it from sinking into the sludge of time. I take one hot shower after another, shave twice a day, listen to the same old records over and over again. In fact, the out-of-date sounds of Peter, Paul, and Mary are playing behind me right now.

"Don't think twice, it's all right."

▶ **31**

The following day, I invited the Rat to the swimming pool of the hillside hotel at the top of the town. It was the end of summer, and the pool was somewhat hard to get to, so only about ten people were there, half of them American guests more intent on soaking up the rays than on doing any real swimming.

The hotel had originally been the villa of a prewar aristocratic family. It boasted a beautiful garden with a sprawling lawn, and if you walked up the slope, along the rose hedge that set the pool apart from the main building, you came to a small hill that provided a striking view of the ocean, the harbor, and the town.

The Rat and I raced a few lengths in the twenty-five-meter

pool before settling back in deck chairs with a pair of cold Cokes. I caught my breath and lit up a smoke, while the Rat watched a little American girl paddling around by herself in the water.

The sky was clear and blue, and crisscrossed by the frozen white trails of jets that could still be seen on the horizon.

"Feels like there used to be more airplanes when we were young, doesn't it," said the Rat, looking up at the sky. "Of course, most were American military planes. Like those twin-fuselage propeller jobs. Remember?"

"You mean P-38s?"

"No, the ones I'm talking about were transport planes. A lot bigger than P-38s. Sometimes they'd fly so low you could see the Air Force insignia . . . And I can remember DC-6s, DC-7s, even Sabre jets."

"That's really going back."

"Yeah, back to Eisenhower's time. When a U.S. Navy cruiser came into port the whole town crawled with sailors and MPs. You ever see an MP?"

"Yeah."

"So many things have disappeared. Not that I cared much for the soldiers."

I nodded.

"The Sabres were great planes. Except they dropped napalm. You ever see what napalm does?"

"In war movies."

"Humans come up with all kinds of stuff. Really well-made stuff, too. Who knows, in another ten years we may be feeling nostalgic about napalm."

I laughed and lit a second cigarette. "You into planes?"

"I used to dream of being a pilot. My eyes are bad, though, so I had to give it up."

"Really?"

"I love the sky. I could look at it forever, but when I don't want to I don't have to."

The Rat fell silent for five minutes. Then all of a sudden he started up again.

"Sometimes I feel I can't take it anymore," he said. "The whole thing about being rich. I just want to escape. You know the feeling?"

"How the hell would I?" His naïveté was astonishing. "Still, you should get out. If you really want to, that is."

"That could be the answer, you know. Find some town I've never heard of. Start all over from scratch. Not a bad idea."

"What about school?"

"I dropped out. Couldn't go back if I wanted to."

From behind his sunglasses, the Rat's eyes were following the little girl, still paddling happily by herself in the pool.

"Why'd you quit?"

"I guess I was fed up with the whole thing. But I gave it my best shot. Surprised myself, really. I learned to think about people other than me, but in the end I just got kicked around by a cop. The way I see it, sooner or later everyone returns to his post. Except yours truly. For me, it was a game of musical chairs—there was no place I could call my own."

"So what'll you do now?"

The Rat toweled off his feet.

"I might write a novel," he said a moment later. "What do you think?"

"I think it's a great idea."

The Rat nodded.

"What kind of novel?"

"A good novel. From where I stand, anyway. I doubt I have any special talent for writing, but if I stick with it at least I can become more enlightened. Otherwise, what's the point, right?"

"Right."

"So the novel will be for myself. Or maybe for the cicadas."

"The cicadas?"

"Yeah."

The Rat toyed with the Kennedy half-dollar pendant dangling on his bare chest.

"I went to Nara a few years ago with a girl. It was scorching hot, and we were hiking in the hills for about three hours. We didn't bump into any people, just wild birds that flew away screeching. There were big brown cicadas shrilling on their backs on the paths between the paddy fields—that sort of place. It was so hot.

"Anyway, we found a nice breezy place to stop, a grassy slope where we could sit and mop off the sweat. There was a broad, deep moat at the foot of the slope, and beyond that a round, tree-covered hill that looked like an island. It was an ancient burial mound, the grave of an emperor. Ever seen one of those?"

I nodded.

"It set me to thinking. Like, why build something so enormous? Of course, all graves mean something. Everyone dies, and so on. We learn from them. But this tomb was just too big. When something is that huge it changes everything around it. To be blunt, it didn't look like a tomb at all. It was a small mountain. The surface of the moat was covered with frogs and weeds, and the fence was a mass of spider webs. So I was sitting there looking at the burial mound and listening to the breeze coming across the water. And I felt this emotion I can't put into words. No, emotion isn't right. It's more like an awareness of being enveloped by something. It's as if the cicadas and frogs and spiders and wind and everything else were one single entity flowing through the cosmos."

The Rat paused to swallow the last of his by-now-flat Coke.

"So whenever I write, I keep that summer afternoon and the tree-covered burial mound in mind. And I think, what could be cooler than writing something for the cicadas and frogs and spiders, and the summer grasses and the wind?"

His story complete, the Rat folded his hands behind his head and looked up at the sky.

"So then, have you tried writing anything?"

"No, not a line. Can't write a damn thing."

"Really?"

"Ye are the salt of the earth."

I was silent.

"But if the salt have lost its savor, wherewith shall it be salted?" the Rat intoned.

When evening came and the shadows lengthened, the Rat and I moved from the pool to the small hotel bar, where they were playing Mantovani's versions of Italian folk songs, and we drank cold beer. The lights of the harbor sparkled in the big windows.

"So what's the story with the girl?" I finally worked up the nerve to ask him.

The Rat wiped the foam from his mouth with the back of his hand and studied the ceiling as if pondering something.

"To be frank, I decided not to share that with you. It's just a load of crap."

"But you did try to talk to me about it before."

"That's true. But I changed my mind. There are things in this world you can't do a damn thing about."

"Like what?"

"Like a rotten tooth, for example. One day it just starts aching. No one can ease the pain, no matter how hard they try to comfort you. It makes you furious with yourself. Next thing you know you're furious with them because they aren't pissed off with themselves. See how it escalates?"

"Sort of," I said. "But try to think it through a little further. All of us are laboring under the same conditions. It's like we're all flying in the same busted airplane. Sure, some of us are luckier than others. Some are tough and some are weak. Some are rich and some poor. But no one's superman—in that way, we're all weak. If we own things, we're terrified we'll lose them; if we've got nothing we worry it'll be that way forever. *We're all the same.* If you catch on to that early enough, you can try to make yourself stronger, even if only a little. It's okay to fake it. Right? There are no truly strong people. Only people who pretend to be strong."

"Can I ask one question?"

I nodded.

"In all honesty, do you believe what you just said?"

"Sure I do."

The Rat studied his glass for a minute.

"Do me a favor and tell me you're lying," he said, in all seriousness.

I dropped the Rat off at his house and continued on alone to J's Bar.

"Were you able to talk to him?"

"Yeah, I talked to him."

"I'm glad," J said, putting a plate of fries in front of me.

▶ **32**

Derek Hartfield was a prolific writer; yet despite his massive body of work, he seldom spoke of life, dreams, or love. In his semi-autobiographical *One and a Half Times Around the Rainbow* (1937)—one of his more serious efforts (in that it featured no aliens or monsters)—Hartfield seems to have little in mind beyond jokes, sarcasm, paradox, and vitriol. Yet there is a brief passage that reveals something of what he felt in reality:

> I swear with my hand on this room's most sacred book, the alphabetized telephone directory, to speak the honest truth. Namely, that human existence is a hollow sham. And that, yes, salvation is possible. In the very beginning our hollowness was incomplete. It is we who completed it through unstinting effort, piling one struggle on top of another until every last shred of meaning was worn away. I have no intention of using my writing to detail each painstaking step in this erosion. That would be a waste of my time. Those of you who want to read about that should turn to Romain Rolland's *Jean-Christophe*. It is all written there.

Hartfield's staunch admiration for *Jean-Christophe* was based on two things: first, that it provided a strict chronological and detailed record of the life of a single man, from birth to death; and second, on top of that, that it was dreadfully long. In Hartfield's cherished opinion, literature should be understood as information, quantifiable through graphs, chronological charts, and the like; its accuracy was therefore proportionate to its volume.

Hartfield was always critical of Tolstoy's *War and Peace*. Its length, he wrote, could hardly be faulted. Yet its failure to incorporate what he termed Cosmic Ideas gave him an impression of incoherence. We can take "Cosmic Ideas" to mean "sterility."

Hartfield's favorite book was *A Dog of Flanders*. "Can you believe," he is quoted as saying, "that a dog would really give up its life for a painting?"

Hartfield was asked the following in a newspaper interview.

"In your most recent novel, your hero, Waldo, dies twice on Mars and then once again on Venus. Isn't that contradictory?"

"Are you familiar," Hartfield replied, "with how time flows in cosmic space?"

"No," the reporter answered. "But then no one else is, either."

"What would be the point of writing a novel about things everyone already knows?"

*

The short story "The Martian Wells" stands apart from Hartfield's other works, setting the stage for the emergence of Ray Bradbury. I read it a long time ago, so many of the details escape me, but here is a rough summary:

"The Martian Wells" tells the story of a young man who

explores the many bottomless wells of the planet Mars. Although it is known that the wells were dug tens of thousands of years ago, strangely, the Martians took care to ensure that none had any contact with water. What, then, was their purpose? No one knows. The wells were all the Martians left behind—nothing else remains. No written language, no dwellings, no eating implements, no metal, no graves, no rockets, no cities, no vending machines, not even a seashell. Only the wells. Earthling scientists debate whether or not the Martians possessed anything that could be termed a civilization; yet their wells were so finely constructed that even after tens of thousands of years, they remain in perfect shape, not a brick out of place. Adventurers and scientific explorers attempt to investigate these wells. Yet those who use ropes retreat when they find the wells too deep and their side passages too extensive, while those who venture down without ropes never make it back to the surface.That is, until the young man appears. A cosmic wanderer, he has wearied of the vastness of outer space and desires only to die an anonymous death. As he descends into one of the wells, however, his state of mind improves, and a curious power takes hold of his body. About half a mile down, he finds a promising tunnel and decides to follow its twisting path to wherever it may lead. On his way, he loses track of time. His watch has stopped. He may have been walking for two hours or two days. Yet, embraced by the strange power, he feels neither hunger nor fatigue.

Then, all of a sudden, he feels the light of the sun. His tunnel has intersected with another well. He scrambles to the surface. Sitting on the well's rim, he gazes out over an unbroken wilderness, then up at the sun. Something has changed. The smell of the wind, the sun . . . the sun is above his head, yet it looks as if it were setting, a huge orange lump suspended in the sky.

"In another 250,000 years the sun will explode," a voice whispers. "Click . . . OFF! 250,000 years. Not so far away, you know."

It is the voice of the wind.

"Don't mind me. I'm just the wind. You can call me Martian if you wish. The word has a nice ring to it. Not that words mean anything to me."

"But you're speaking."

"Me? No, the words are yours. I'm just sending hints to your mind."

"But what has happened to the sun?"

"It got old. It's dying. There's nothing either of us can do about it."

"But it's so sudden . . ."

"Sudden? Hardly. One and a half billion years passed while you were down the well. As you earthlings say, time flies. The tunnels you passed through run along a time warp—that's why we dug them as we did. They allow us to wander across time. From the creation of the universe to its final demise. We exist in a realm outside life and death. We are the wind."

"May I ask one question?"

"Certainly."

"What have you learned?"

The air around him shook as the wind laughed. Then eternal silence descended once more to the Martian plain. The young man took a revolver from his pocket, placed it to his temple, and squeezed the trigger.

▸ **33**

The telephone rang.

"I'm back," she said.

"Can I see you?"

"Are you free right now?"

"Sure."

"Okay, then make it five o'clock, in front of the YWCA."

"What're you doing at the YWCA?"

"French class."

"French?"

"*Oui!*"

I hung up, took a shower, and had a beer. I was polishing it off when it began to pour outside.

The rain had stopped by the time I reached the YWCA, yet the girls leaving the front gate regarded the sky with deep suspicion, opening and closing their umbrellas as they emerged. I pulled up across the street, cut the engine, and lit a cigarette. The gate's rain-drenched columns loomed like a pair of black gravestones in a wasteland. An office building had been thrown up next to the dingy YWCA; its newness made it appear even cheaper, and an enormous sign advertising refrigerators was perched on its roof. It showed a thirtyish, apron-clad, anemic-looking woman stooping to open the door of her fridge with what appeared to be great delight, providing a view of its contents.

The freezer compartment contained an ice tray, a quart of vanilla ice cream, and a package of frozen shrimp; the next section down held a carton of eggs, a box of butter, Camembert cheese, and a boneless ham; the level below that contained fish and chicken legs; the plastic crisper at the very bottom was stocked with tomatoes, cucumbers, asparagus, lettuce, and grapefruit, while arranged on the inside of the door were three bottles each of cola and beer, and a carton of milk.

I sat there leaning on the steering wheel, imagining the best order in which to polish off all that food. I was thwarted by the ice cream, far more than I could possibly manage, and the fatal absence of salad dressing.

She came out of the gate just after five. Her hair was pulled back in a ponytail and she was wearing a pink Lacoste polo shirt, a white cotton miniskirt, and glasses. She looked as if she had aged three years in a week. Maybe it was the new hairstyle and the glasses.

"Darn that rain!" she said, sliding into the passenger's seat and nervously straightening her skirt.

"You get wet?"

"A little."

I grabbed the beach towel that had lain untouched on the backseat since my last trip to the swimming pool and handed it to her. She wiped the sweat from her face and patted her wet hair a number of times before handing it back to me.

"I was having coffee just around the corner when the rain started. It was a real downpour."

"At least it cooled things off."

"Yeah," she nodded, sticking her arm out the window to test the temperature. There was a new awkwardness between us.

"Have a good trip?" I asked.

"There was no trip. I lied to you."

"Why would you do that?"

"I'll tell you later."

▶ **34**

I do tell lies on occasion. The last time was a year ago.

Lies are terrible things. One could say that the greatest sins afflicting modern society are the proliferation of lies and silence. We lie through our teeth, then swallow our tongues.

All the same, were we to speak only the truth all year round, then the truth might lose its value.

Last year, my girlfriend and I were snuggling together in bed. We were famished.

"Is there anything to eat?" I asked her.

"Let me check."

She walked naked to the fridge, found some sausage, lettuce, and stale bread, and threw together two sandwiches, which she brought back to bed with two cups of instant coffee. It was a chilly night for October; by the time she slipped back under the covers she was as cold as a can of salmon.

"No mustard, I'm afraid."

"Fine by me."

We curled up together and watched an old movie on TV as we munched on the sandwiches.

It was *The Bridge on the River Kwai*.

She was moved by the scene at the end, where they blow up the bridge.

"Then why did they work so hard to build it?" she sighed, pointing at Alec Guinness, who was standing transfixed by the sight.

"Out of pride."

"Mmph," she responded, her cheeks stuffed with bread, as she contemplated the nature of human pride. Then, as always, I had no idea at all what was going on inside her head.

"Do you love me?"

"Sure I do."

"Enough to marry me?"

"Right away?"

"Someday. In the future."

"Sure I want to marry you."

"But you never said anything until I asked."

"It slipped my mind."

"How many kids do you want?"

"Three."

"Boys? Girls?"

"Two girls and a boy."

She took a swallow of coffee to wash down the rest of the bread, and looked me square in the eye.

"LIAR!" she said.

But she was wrong. I had lied only once.

▶ **35**

The girl with nine fingers and I went to a small restaurant near the port for a simple meal, followed by a Bloody Mary and a bourbon.

"Do you want to know what actually happened?" she asked.

"You know, last year we dissected a cow."

"For real?"

"When we cut open its abdomen all it contained was a single cud. So I put the cud in a plastic bag, took it home, and set it on my desk. Since then, whenever things get rough, I look at that lump of half-digested grass and wonder, why would a cow take such pains to regurgitate and chew such an unappetizing, pathetic thing over and over again?"

She pursed her lips in a half smile and studied my face for a moment.

"I get it," she said. "I won't say another word about it."

I nodded.

"There's something I wanted to ask you," she said. "Is that okay?"

"Go ahead."

"Why do people die?"

"Because of evolution. An individual organism can't sustain the amount of energy that evolution requires; evolution has to work its way through generations. That's just one theory, of course."

"So are we still evolving?"

"Bit by bit."

"Why is that necessary?"

"Opinions are divided on that, too. The only thing we know for sure is that the universe itself is evolving. We can't tell if it's heading in any particular direction, or if some greater force is intervening, but we do know that evolution is for real, and that we are only a part of the process." I set my bourbon down and lit a cigarette.

"No one knows where that energy comes from," I said.

"Really?"

"Really."

She stirred the ice in her drink with her finger and studied the white tablecloth.

"I guess a hundred years after my death no one will remember I ever existed."

"Probably not," I said.

·   ·   ·

We left the restaurant and strolled along the quiet street past the row of warehouses. It was twilight, and everything was strangely vivid. As I walked beside her, I caught the faint fragrance of her shampoo. The wind that shook the leaves of the willow trees had a trace of the end of summer. We had not been walking long when she reached down and took my hand in hers. It was the hand with five fingers.

"When are you going back to Tokyo?"

"Next week. I've got to take a test."

She remained silent.

"I'll be back in the winter. Before Christmas. My birthday's on December 24th."

She nodded. She seemed to have something else on her mind.

"So you're a Capricorn?" she said.

"Yes. How about you?"

"The same. January 10th."

"Not the best sign to be born under, huh? Like Jesus Christ."

"That's true," she said, adjusting her grip on my hand. "I think I'll miss you when you're gone."

"We'll meet again for sure."

She said nothing.

The warehouses we passed looked quite old, the cracks between the bricks slick with green moss, the darkened windows high above covered by sturdy iron grating. A sign with the name of the trading company was attached to each of the rusted doors. Where the line of warehouses broke off, the full aroma of the ocean hit us and the row of willows abruptly ended, as if teeth had been knocked from their sockets. We continued across the overgrown tracks of the harbor line and onto the deserted pier, where we sat on the stone steps of one of the warehouses facing the ocean.

The lights of the shipyard dock were straight ahead, illuminating a Greek freighter whose cargo had already been unloaded, judging from the high waterline. The freighter looked abandoned; its white-painted deck was rusted red by the salt wind, and its flanks were caked with barnacles, like a sick man's scabs.

We sat there for a very long time, just looking at the ocean, the evening sky, and the ship while the sea breeze blew through the trembling grass. As the dusk softened to night, a handful of stars began to twinkle above the dock.

She was the one who broke the silence, pounding her left fist into her right hand again and again until the palm was quite red. She stared at it with dull eyes, as if she'd lost all interest all of a sudden.

"I hate everybody." The words hung in isolation.

"Even me?"

"Sorry." Blushing, she returned her hands to her knees, as if trying to pull herself together. "I don't hate you."

"Not so much anyway, right?"

She nodded and gave me a faint smile. When she lit her cigarette I could see her hands tremble. The smoke rode the ocean wind past her hair and vanished in the darkness.

"When I'm sitting alone, all these voices start speaking to me," she said. "All sorts of people—ones I know, ones I don't know, my father, my mother, my teachers."

I nodded.

"Most of what they say is awful. They tell me to drop dead, or say really filthy things."

"What kind of things?"

"I can't repeat them."

She crushed the cigarette she had just lit with her leather sandal, and gently pressed her eyes with her fingertips.

"Do you think I'm sick?"

"It's hard to say." I shook my head to show her that I really had no idea. "If you're worried you should go see a doctor."

"Don't worry—I'll be okay."

She lit a second cigarette and tried to laugh, but couldn't pull it off.

"You're the first person I've ever told about this."

I took her hand in mine. It was quivering, and a clammy sweat oozed from between her fingers.

"I really didn't want to lie to you."

"I know."

We fell quiet again, listening to the soft sound of the waves lapping against the pier. Time went by, more time than I can recall.

Before I knew it she was crying. I traced the line of her tear-soaked cheek with my finger and wrapped my arm around her shoulder.

It had been a long time since I felt the fragrance of summer: the scent of the ocean, a distant train whistle, the touch of a girl's skin, the lemony perfume of her hair, the evening wind, faint glimmers of hope, summer dreams.

But none of these were the way they once had been; they were all somehow off, as if copied with tracing paper that kept slipping out of place.

▸ **36**

It took us half an hour to walk to her apartment. The night was perfect, and crying had left her in a surprisingly good mood. We stopped at several shops on the way and bought a whole bunch of useless stuff—strawberry-flavored toothpaste, a gaudy beach towel, jigsaw puzzles made in Denmark, a six-color ballpoint pen, and so on—all of which we toted up the slope, pausing every so often to look back at the harbor.

"Is it okay to leave your car back there?"

"I'll get it later."

"Can't it wait till morning?"

"No problem," I said. We continued our stroll up the flag-stone path.

"I really don't want to be alone tonight," she said to the flagstones.

I nodded.

"But you won't be able to polish your father's shoes."

"He can polish them himself every once in a while."

"But will he?"

"Sure. After all, he's a man of principle."

It was a quiet night.

She rolled over to face me, her nose touching my shoulder.

"I'm cold."

"Cold? It's ninety degrees!"

"I don't care. I'm still cold."

I drew the terry-cloth blanket we had tossed near our feet over our shoulders and embraced her. She was shaking like a leaf.

"Are you feeling sick?"

She shook her head.

"I'm scared," she said.

"Of what?"

"Of everything. Aren't you?"

"Not particularly."

She fell quiet. She seemed to be weighing my answer in the palm of her hand.

"Do you want to have sex with me?"

"Uh-huh."

"I can't tonight. I'm sorry."

I nodded, my arms still around her.

"I just had an operation."

"An abortion?"

"Yes."

Her arms slackened around my body, and her fingertips began to describe circles on my shoulder.

"It's weird. I can't remember a thing."

"About what?"

"About him. The father. Can't even remember what he looked like."

I ran my palm over her hair.

"I thought I loved him. For a moment, anyway." She paused. "Have you ever been in love?"

"Uh-huh."

"Can you remember what she looked like?"

I tried to call to mind the faces of the three girls I had slept with, but, strange to say, I couldn't form a clear picture of a single one.

"No," I said.

"Weird, huh? Why is it like this?"

"Probably because it makes it easier."

She nodded several times, her face lying sideways, in profile, on my bare chest.

"You know, if you're too horny we can find another way to . . ."

"No. I'm okay."

"Really?"

"Yeah."

Her arms tightened again around my back. I could feel her breasts pressing against the pit of my stomach. I was dying for a beer.

"For years now, a lot of things haven't gone right for me."

"How many years?"

"Twelve, thirteen . . . since my dad got sick. I can't remember a single thing before that. Everything is screwed up. It's like I'm caught in an ill wind."

"Winds change direction."

"You really think so?"

"If you wait long enough, yes."

She said nothing. Her silence was as dry as a desert; it swallowed my words, leaving a bitter taste in my mouth.

"I tried to believe that," she said. "But it never worked. I tried to fall in love, and I tried to hang on and be patient. But still . . ."

We didn't attempt to talk after that, just held on to each other. She lay there motionless, as if fast asleep, her head on my chest, her lips grazing my nipple.

Her silence lasted a long time. A very long time. I lay there in a half-conscious state, gazing at the dark ceiling.

.   .   .

"Mama," she murmured, as if in a dream. She was fast asleep, no question about it.

▸ 37

Hey, all you out there. How're you feeling tonight? It's Saturday evening again, time for your *Greatest Hits Request Show*, right here on NEB Radio. For the next two hours we're going to play all your favorite tunes. But first, the end of summer is right around the corner. How about it, guys—was your summer a good one?

I'm gonna shake things up a little tonight, read you a letter I just received from one of our listeners before we start the music. So here goes.

How are you?

I love your program and look forward to it every week. Everything moves so fast—this fall marks my third year here in the hospital. How quickly time passes! Of course, the change of seasons doesn't mean very much for someone like me, who lives in an air-conditioned room and can barely glimpse what lies outside her window, but all the same it fills me with delight to imagine the season passing and a new one coming to take its place.

I am seventeen years old, and for the past three years I have been unable to read a book or watch TV or go out for a walk . . . or get out of bed or roll over, for that matter. In fact, I am dictating this letter to my older sister, who has been with me all this time. She dropped out of university to look after me. Of course I am very grateful to her. What lying here in bed for the past three years has taught me is that, however miserable your situation, there is always something to learn, and that helps me go on living one day at a time.

I am told my illness is a neurological disease affecting the spinal cord. It's a real downer, but of course there is hope for a cure. Still, the odds are low, just three percent . . . According to my doctor (a really cool guy), that is the figure one gets looking at the recovery rate of others with the same disease. He says this means my chances are better than a rookie pitching a no-hitter against the Tokyo Giants, but not as good as him shutting them out.

It terrifies me to think what might await me. So much so that sometimes I feel like screaming. To lie like a rock in this bed staring at the ceiling for decades—never reading books or walking in the wind, never being loved by anybody—and then to die alone, an old woman. It is just too sad. Sometimes, when I wake at three in the morning, I think I can hear my spine melting away bit by bit. It may not be my imagination, either.

No more unpleasantness. As my sister reminds me hundreds of times a day, I must try to think only positive thoughts. That and sleep well at night. Night is when the bad thoughts tend to visit.

The harbor is visible from my window. Every morning I picture how great it would be to get out of bed, walk down to the waterfront, and fill my lungs with ocean air. If I could do that even once, perhaps then I could begin to understand why the world is as it is. That's the way I feel. And if I could gain even a shred of that understanding, maybe I could bear the idea of dying in this bed.

All the best.

She didn't sign her name.

I received this letter a little after three o'clock yesterday afternoon, and read it while having my coffee in our studio lounge. In the evening, I walked down to the harbor after work and looked up at the mountains. Listen, my young friend, you say the harbor is visible from your window, so I should be able to see your window from the harbor too. So many lights were shining up there on the mountainside. I couldn't tell which one of them was yours, of course. Some lights shone from poor people's houses, some from the mansions of the wealthy. There were the lights of hotels, of schools, of companies. So many people, so many ways of life. I had never thought about it like that before. It brought tears to my eyes. I hadn't cried in a dog's age. But don't get me wrong, my young friend. I wasn't crying out of sympathy for you. No, it was for another reason. Listen, all of you, I'm only going to tell you once. This is it:

I love all you kids out there!

If you remember anything about this program in ten years— the songs I played for you, perhaps, or maybe even yours truly—then please remember that.

So here's her request. Elvis Presley's "Good Luck Charm." When this song is over, I'll go back for the next one hour and fifty minutes to being your canine stand-up comedian, as always.

Thanks for tuning in.

▸ **38**

The evening I left for Tokyo, I stopped by J's Bar, suitcase in hand. It was before opening time, but J let me in and gave me a beer.

"I'm taking the night bus," I told him. He nodded several times as he peeled the potatoes for that evening.

"It's going to be lonely around here with you gone. You and the Rat made quite a team," he said, pointing at the print above the counter. "He'll miss you too."

"Yeah."

"You like Tokyo?"

"One place or another—it's all the same to me."

"I guess so. I haven't left this town once since the Tokyo Olympics."

"You like it here?"

"As you said. It's all the same."

"Yeah."

"I'd love to go back to China in a few years' time, though. Not that I've ever been there, of course. Crosses my mind every time I go down to the harbor and see the ships."

"My uncle died in China."

"I see. All kinds of people died there. Still, we're all brothers."

J treated me to a few more rounds. Then to top it off, he gave me a plastic bag of fries fresh from the fryer to take with me.

"Thanks."

"My pleasure. You guys grew up so fast. First time I saw you, you were in high school."

I smiled and nodded.

"Goodbye," I said.

"Take care," J said.

.   .   .

The daily proverb for August 26 on the calendar in J's Bar read, "He who gives freely shall receive in kind."

I bought my ticket for the night bus and sat down on a bench in the waiting area where I could see the town's lights. As the night deepened, the lights went out one by one until at last only the streetlights and neon signs were left. A distant foghorn brought with it a faint sea breeze.

The bus door was flanked by two workers checking tickets and seat numbers. When I handed one my ticket, he announced, "Row 21, China."

"China?" I asked.

"That means 21C. We go by the first letter. America is 'A,' Brazil is 'B,' China is 'C,' and Denmark is 'D.' If my partner doesn't catch what I'm saying," he said, pointing to the other guy who was ticking off the numbers, "then we've got a problem."

Nodding, I boarded the bus, found my seat, and settled back to enjoy my still-warm fries.

All things pass. None of us can manage to hold on to anything.

In that way, we live our lives.

▶ **39**

This is the end of my story. Of course there is a sequel.

.　　.　　.

I've already turned twenty-nine, the Rat thirty. Getting up there. J's Bar was renovated when they widened his street, turning it into a thoroughly chic café. Nevertheless, J still peels a bucket of potatoes every day and passes his time sipping beer and grumbling about how much better the customers were back in the old days.

I got married, and we live in Tokyo.

My wife and I are big Sam Peckinpah fans; we go see his films when they come out and then drink two beers each and feed popcorn to the pigeons in Hibiya Park on the way home. My favorite is *Bring Me the Head of Alfredo Garcia*, hers is *Convoy*. Of the films not by Peckinpah, I like *Ashes and Diamonds*, while she likes *Mother Joan of the Angels*, both Polish films. I guess your tastes come to resemble each other's when you've been living together a long time.

If someone asked me if I was happy, I guess I would have to say yes. Dreams are like that in the end.

The Rat is still writing novels. He sends me photocopies each Christmas. Last year it was the story of a cook working at a mental hospital; the year before, it was about a comic band that modeled themselves on the Brothers Karamazov. As always, there is no sex, and none of the characters dies.

On the first page he always writes:

> "Happy Birthday
> and
> White Christmas"

That's because my birthday is December 24th.

.　　.　　.

I never saw the girl with four fingers on her left hand again. When I returned to the town that winter, she had quit the record shop and vacated her apartment. She vanished without a trace, swept away by the flow of time and its flood of people.

When I go back to the town in summer, I walk the same streets we did and sit on the stone steps of the same warehouse and look at the ocean. Sometimes I want to cry, but the tears don't come. It's that kind of a thing.

"California Girls" still sits in the corner of my record shelf. When summer comes I dust it off and play it over and over again. I sit back, have a beer, and think about California.

Adjacent to my record collection is my desk, above which hangs a dried hunk of mummified grass. The cud I took from that cow's stomach.

My photograph of the French literature major who died got lost in the shuffle when I moved.

The Beach Boys came out with a new album, their first in a long time.

I wish they all could be
California girls . . .

▸ 40

To wrap up, let me talk a little more about Derek Hartfield.

Hartfield was born (in 1909) and raised in a small Ohio town. His father was a quiet man who worked as a telegraph operator, his mother a plump woman who loved astrology and baked delicious cookies. Hartfield himself was a gloomy, friendless child who spent his free time absorbed in reading comic books and pulp magazines, and eating his mother's cookies. After graduating from high school, he tried working at the post office in his hometown, but quickly gave that up to concentrate on what he had come to realize was the only path for him, his true vocation—writing novels.

He sold the fifth story he wrote to *Weird Tales* for the sum of twenty dollars in 1930. During the subsequent year he wrote at a clip of 70,000 words per month, a pace he raised to 100,000 words the following year and to 150,000 by the year before his death. Legend has it that he had to buy a new Remington typewriter every six months.

Almost everything Hartfield wrote was either an adventure or a horror story; his biggest hit, the series *Waldo, Boy Adventurer*, an inspired mixture of the two, totaled forty-two volumes. In the course of the series, Waldo died 3 times, killed 5,000 enemies, and made love to a total of 375 women, including one Martian. A number of the Waldo stories can be read in Japanese translation.

Hartfield detested so many things: post offices, high schools, publishing houses, carrots, women, dogs—the list is endless. There were only three things that he liked, namely, guns, cats, and his mother's cookies. Apart from Paramount Pictures and the FBI testing center, he seems to have owned the most extensive gun collection in the United States. The only firearms he didn't collect were anti-aircraft and anti-tank weapons. His most prized piece was a .38 revolver with a pearl-studded handle. He kept just a single bullet in its chamber, and liked to boast, "I'll use this baby to revolve myself someday."

Yet when his mother died in 1938, he traveled all the way to New York to jump off the Empire State Building, flattening himself like a frog on the pavement below.

Following his wishes, this quote from Nietzsche was carved on his gravestone:

How can those who live in the light of day possibly comprehend the depths of night?

MAY 1979

 PINBALL, 1973

I enjoyed listening to stories about faraway places so much that it became a kind of sickness.

Back then, a good ten years ago now, I went around asking everyone to tell me about where they were born and raised. In those days there must have been a real shortage of good listeners, because everyone I approached talked to me with great enthusiasm. When rumor got out about what I was doing, people I'd never laid eyes on started showing up just to tell me their stories.

They rambled on and on about anything and everything, as if tossing stones into a dry well, then left feeling satisfied. Some told their stories in high spirits, others in anger. There were stories that felt clear and direct, and other stories that seemed pointless from start to finish. There were boring stories, sob stories, and tongue-in-cheek, off-the-wall stories. Always, though, I listened to what they had to say as attentively as I could.

For whatever reason, they all seemed compelled to get their story out—if not to a specific person, then to the world at large.

It made me think of a cardboard box packed with monkeys. I would extract one monkey after another, carefully dust it off, slap it on the bum, and release it into the fields. I had no idea what happened to the monkeys after that. Probably they spent their lives gnawing on acorns somewhere, then died off. Such was their fate.

Truth be told, it was a laborious task, with little reward. Had a contest been held that year to determine the World's Best Listener, I would have won hands down. My prize? Probably a box of kitchen matches.

One of the people who talked to me came from Saturn, while another was from Venus. Their stories were especially memorable. I'll quote the guy from Saturn first.

"It's f-freezing cold . . . up there," he groaned. "Just thinking about it drives me n-nuts."

He belonged to the radical group occupying Building Nine on our campus. Their motto was "Action determines ideology, not vice versa." What determined action was never made clear to me, though I asked. Building Nine was equipped with a water cooler, a telephone, a hot-water heater, and, on the second floor, a really cool music room with two thousand records and Altec A5 speakers. Compared to other occupied buildings on campus (like Building Eight, which stank like a bicycle racetrack toilet), it was paradise. The group shaved with hot water every morning, made all the long-distance phone calls they wanted in the afternoon, and gathered to listen to records in the evening. By the time autumn came around they were all classical music aficionados.

Is it true that they were blissing out to Vivaldi's "Il cimento dell'armonia e dell'invenzione" at full blast when the riot police's third division came crashing into Building Nine that perfect cloudless November day? Whether fact or fiction, it endures as one of the more heartwarming legends revolving around the year that was 1969.

It was thus to the accompaniment of the distant strains of Haydn's Piano Sonata in G minor that I picked my way under and through the tottering pile of benches that served as a barricade for Building Nine. For some reason it felt nostalgic, as if I were making my way up a camellia-covered slope to visit my girlfriend's home in one of the nicer parts of the city. The guy from Saturn pushed their most comfortable chair in my direction, handed me a beaker filched from the science labs, and filled it with lukewarm beer.

"Gravity is a lot stronger up there," he said, continuing his story. "I know a guy whose foot got crushed when he spat out a wad of chewing gum. It's h-hell!"

"You don't say," I answered. By that time, I had mastered a repertoire of three hundred stock responses that I could draw on to keep my respondents talking.

"The s-sun is tiny, too. Like an orange on home plate seen from center field. So it's always dark," he sighed.

"Then why doesn't everyone leave?" I asked. "There must be nicer planets to live on."

"Beats me. Maybe 'cause they were born there. It's like that. Take me, for example. I'm going home to Saturn when I graduate. To make it a b-better place. It's the r-r-revolution."

Anyway, I just love stories about faraway towns. I stash some of them away in my mind, like a bear preparing for hibernation. If I close my eyes, I can picture the streets, line them with dwellings, hear the voices of the residents. I can even feel the gentle yet unmistakable rhythms of their lives, distant people whose paths I may never cross as long as I live.

Q

On occasion, Naoko would tell me her stories. I can still remember every word.

"I don't know what to call the place," she said in a bored voice, her cheek resting on her hand in the bright sunlight of the student lounge. Then she gave a little laugh. I waited for her to continue. She was a girl who spoke slowly and chose her words with care.

We sat at a red plastic table, a paper cup stuffed with cigarette butts between us. The light streamed through the tall windows like in a Rubens painting, neatly dividing our table down the middle so that my right hand was illuminated and my left was in shade.

It was the spring of 1969, and we were both twenty. New students wearing new shoes, carrying new course catalogs, their heads crammed with new brains, packed the lounge. Throughout our conversation we heard complaints and apologies as people bumped into each other.

"I mean," she continued, "you can't even call it a real town. There's just a railroad track and a station. A pathetic two-bit station the engineer could zip right past in the rain."

I nodded. For a full thirty seconds we sat there in silence, watching the cigarette smoke curl in the sunlight.

"And there's always a dog walking the platform from one end to the other. That kind of station. Got the picture?"

I nodded again.

"When you step out of the station there's a little roundabout and a bus stop. And a few shops . . . Really sleepy-looking places. Go straight from there and you bump into a park. There's a slide and three sets of swings."

"Is there a sandbox?"

"A sandbox?" She thought for a moment before nodding, as if to confirm her recollection. "Yes, there's one of those too."

We fell silent again. I gingerly extinguished my cigarette, which I had smoked down to the butt, in the paper cup.

"It's a nowhere kind of town. Why any place so boring was put on this earth is beyond me."

"God reveals Himself in many forms," I said.

Naoko shook her head and laughed. It was a regular sort of laugh, the kind you'd expect from a girl who had received straight A's in school; yet for some strange reason it lingered long after she had left, like the grin of the Cheshire Cat in *Alice in Wonderland*.

But what excited me most was the thought of meeting the dog that walked up and down the platform.

$$Q$$

Four years later, in May 1973, I did go alone to that station. I wanted to see that dog. In preparation, I shaved, donned a necktie for the first time in six months, and put on a new pair of cordovan shoes.

$$Q$$

I stepped down from the sorry old suburban local train, whose two rusted passenger cars looked ready to disintegrate at any moment, and inhaled the smell of fresh grass. It was a fragrance from picnics long past; even the May breeze seemed to be reaching me from some distant time. When I listened carefully, I could hear skylarks singing overhead.

I let out a long yawn, sat down on a platform bench, and lit up a cigarette in disgust. The energy I had felt when I left my apartment early that morning had vanished. It was the same old thing over and over again. An endless déjà vu that got worse each time around.

At one time in my life I had gone to sleep each night sprawled on the floor with a group of friends. In the morning some guy would step on my head. Sorry, he'd say. Then I'd hear the sound of pissing. The same old thing.

With my cigarette hanging from the corner of my mouth, I loosened my tie and began rubbing the soles of my new shoes back and forth on the concrete platform. I was trying to lessen the pain in my feet. They weren't killing me, but the soreness was making me feel disjointed, as if my body were out of whack.

The dog was nowhere to be seen.

Out of whack . . .

It's a feeling I get a lot. As if I'm trying to put the jumbled pieces of two different puzzles together at the same time. When I get that way my solution is to drink whiskey and go to bed. The next morning, though, I feel even worse. The same old thing.

When I opened my eyes this time, there were two girls, twins, in bed with me, one on each side. I had awakened to a girl beside me many times before, but needless to say, this was the first time I had found myself next to twins. They were fast asleep, their noses touching my shoulders. It was a cloudless Sunday morning.

A short while later, they woke up at almost the same time, shimmied into the T-shirts and jeans they had dropped beside the bed, trooped into the kitchen without a word, brewed coffee, made toast, took butter out of the fridge, and spread everything out on the table. Not a move was wasted—it looked as if they'd been doing this for years. Outside my window, some kind of bird was perched on the chain-link fence that encircled the golf course, rattling away like a machine gun.

"So what are your names?" I asked the girls. I was in rough shape—my head was splitting.

"They're not much, as names go," said the one sitting on my right.

"That's a fact," said the one on my left. "Just about useless. Know what I mean?"

"Sure," I said.

We sat there at the table, them on one side, me on the other, nibbling our toast and sipping our coffee. Terrific coffee, too.

"Will it be a hassle, us not having names?" one of them asked.

"I don't know."

They thought about it for a while.

"If we need names," the other suggested, "why don't you choose them for us?"

"Call us what you like."

First one would speak, then the other. Like a sound check for a stereo broadcast. My headache was getting worse.

"For example?" I asked.

"Right and left," said one.

"Horizontal and vertical," said the other.

"Up and down."

"Front and back."

"East and west."

"Entrance and exit," I managed to interject, not to be outdone. They looked at each other and burst into satisfied laughter.

Where there is an entrance, there is usually an exit. That's the way things are made. Mailboxes, vacuum cleaners, zoos, salt shakers. Of course there are exceptions. Mousetraps, for instance.

Q

I put out a mousetrap once, under the sink in my apartment. For bait I used peppermint gum. I tried to locate something better, but that was the closest thing to food I came across. The gum was in one of the pockets of my winter coat, along with a movie ticket stub.

On the third morning I found a small mouse caught by its leg in the trap. It was still young, the color of the cashmere sweaters you see piled in London's duty-free shops. Probably fifteen or sixteen in human years. A tender age. Beneath its feet lay a shred of gum.

The mouse had been snared, but I was clueless about what to do with it. By the morning of the fourth day it was dead, its hind leg still pinned. As I looked at its body, I realized one of life's important lessons.

All things should have both an entrance and an exit. That's just the way it is.

Q

The tracks followed a row of hills in a line so straight it looked as if it had been drawn with a ruler. In the distance, like a crumpled piece of paper, I could make out a dark green thicket of trees. The rails gleamed dully in the sun all the way out to that point, then disappeared into the green. It seemed as though the landscape would continue like that for eternity, however far one went. The idea depressed me. If that's how it was, give me the subway any day.

I finished my cigarette, stretched, and gazed up at the sky. I hadn't looked at the sky for some time. In fact, it had been a long while since my eyes had rested on anything.

Not a cloud was visible. A veil of mist hovered in the air, as often happens in the spring, an elusive membrane waiting to be infiltrated from above by the blue sky. Particles of sunlight fell like fine dust, gathering unnoticed on the ground.

In the warm breeze, the light wavered. The air flowed at a leisurely pace, like a flock of birds flying from tree to tree. It skimmed the wooded slopes along the railroad line, crossed the tracks, and passed through the grove without so much as ruffling a leaf. A cuckoo's sharp cry cut through the gentle light like an arrow and disappeared over the distant ridge. The undulating hills resembled a giant sleeping cat, curled up in a warm pool of time.

Q

The pain in my feet was growing worse.

Q

Now let me tell you about the wells.

Naoko had moved to the area when she was twelve. That was 1961, by the Western calendar. The year Ricky Nelson sang "Hello Mary Lou." At the time there was nothing whatsoever to draw anyone's attention to this peaceful green valley. A few farmhouses, some scattered fields, streams full of crayfish, the single-track train line with a yawn-inducing station, and that was it. Most of the farmhouses had persimmon trees growing in their yards, and off in a corner you could usually find a tottering, weather-beaten shed. Nailed to the side of the shed facing the train tracks were sheets of tin with garish painted advertisements for things like toilet paper and soap. That was the kind of place it was, said Naoko. No one even had a dog.

Naoko's family lived in a Western-style two-story house built at the time of the Korean War. Though modestly sized, its pillars were massive and its wood had been chosen with care, so that it looked solid, even dignified. The exterior had been painted three shades of green: exposed to the sun, rain, and wind, the three greens had faded until they matched the color of the surrounding landscape. The grounds were spacious, with several groves of trees and a small pond. Tucked away amid the trees was a snug little structure, an octagonal studio with faded curtains hanging in its bay windows—their original color was anyone's guess. A riotous profusion of narcissus bloomed by the pond, where little birds gathered to splash about in the mornings.

The house had been designed by an old man, an oil painter who had lived there until his lungs gave out the winter before Naoko moved in. That was 1960, the year Bobby Vee sang "Rubber Ball." It rained like crazy that winter. Snow was rare in the area, but the rains were freezing cold. They covered the ground like a chilly blanket and soaked into the soil. All the while, a huge reservoir of sweet mineral water was forming beneath the surface.

The well digger's house was a five-minute walk down the track from the station. It was in a swampy spot close by the river, besieged by mosquitoes and frogs in the summertime. The well digger was a man of about fifty, obstinate and ill-tempered, but a true genius when it came to his craft. He would spend days walking the properties that he had been hired to survey, grumbling to himself and occasionally scooping up a handful of earth and sniffing it. Then, when he was sure he had found the right spot, he would call a couple of his buddies and they would dig straight down until they hit water.

Thus it was that everyone from the area had all the delicious well water they could drink. It was icy cold and so clear you felt you could see through not only the glass but your hand as well. They called it "Fuji snow water," but that was a joke. No way it had come that far.

The fall Naoko turned seventeen, the well digger was killed by a train. The causes of the accident were a driving rain, chilled sake, and partial deafness. The policemen who retrieved the well digger's shredded body—five buckets' worth, in thousands of pieces—from the field had to use long poles with hooks on the end to fend off the wild dogs who descended on the scene. The river swept another bucketful of remains off to various ponds, to become fish food.

Neither of the well digger's two sons wanted to follow in their father's footsteps; both moved out of the area soon after the accident. Nor did anyone else wish to take over the abandoned house, which crumbled bit by bit as the years passed. And so wells which produced that delicious water became harder and harder to find.

I love wells. Whenever I come across one I toss in a pebble. Nothing is more soothing than hearing that small splash rise from the bottom of a deep well.

Q

It was Naoko's father who decided that they would move to the area in 1961. Not only had the dead painter been his close friend; her father was taken by the place itself.

Naoko's father seems to have been a French literary scholar of some note, but around the time she reached school age, without warning, he tossed away his university post to live a life of leisure and indulge his passion: translating enigmatic old French texts, tales of fallen angels and dissolute priests, exorcists and vampires. I don't know all the details. I saw his picture once in a magazine, but that was it. According to Naoko, he had been a real bohemian in his youth. I could get a sense of that by looking at the photo, in which he wore dark glasses and a cap, and was glaring at a spot about a yard above the camera lens. Maybe he had seen something.

Q

There were a number of cultured eccentrics like him in the area when Naoko and her family moved in, a kind of free-floating colony. Like the Siberian penal camps for thought criminals they had back in imperial Russia.

Speaking of penal camps, I remember reading about one of them in a biography of Leon Trotsky. Can't remember much, just the parts about the cockroaches and the reindeer. So let me tell you about the reindeer . . .

Trotsky had stolen a sleigh and a team of four reindeer under cover of darkness and escaped from the penal colony where he had been imprisoned. The reindeer sped madly across the silvery waste. Their breath froze solid in the frigid air; their hooves scattered the virgin snow. When they reached the train station two days later, the exhausted reindeer collapsed, never to rise again. The weeping Trotsky threw his arms around the dead animals and vowed, I will bring justice, truth, and revolution to my country, whatever it takes! Even today, a statue of the four reindeer can be found in Red Square. One is facing east, one north, one west, and one south. Stalin himself couldn't destroy them. If you visit Moscow, go to the square early Saturday morning and watch the junior high school students clean the reindeer with mops. Their red cheeks and white breath are a most refreshing sight.

Back to the other colony.

Its members shunned the flat land near the station, choosing instead to build their wildly idiosyncratic homes on the hillside. Each boasted a garden of preposterous size, preserving the original trees, ponds, and hills. One even had a pretty stream filled with small and tasty sweetfish.

The colony members woke each morning to the turtledove's song and strolled about their gardens over fallen beechnuts, often lifting their eyes to the morning light filtering through the leaves.

But Japan was changing—the Tokyo Olympics were held around this time—and an inexorable wave of urban development was moving toward them. Their homes had overlooked a rich sea of mulberry trees, but now bulldozers were crushing the trees and turning the land black, and a monotonous townscape was taking shape around the train station.

The new residents were by and large mid-level office workers, the ubiquitous salarymen. They leapt out of bed at five o'clock in the morning, splashed water on their faces, and crammed themselves into commuter trains, returning half dead late at night.

And so it was only on Sunday afternoons that they were able to look around at their homes and their community. At the same time, as if by mutual agreement, they all took to raising dogs. The dogs started mating with each other, producing puppies that, in turn, went wild. When Naoko said there were no dogs back in the old days, this is what she meant.

Q

I spent a full hour waiting for the dog to show up. I smoked ten cigarettes in the process, crushing each butt with my foot. I walked to the middle of the platform to drink from the spigot; the icy water was delicious. Still no dog.

A large pond sat next to the station. It snaked like a winding river that had been dammed, with tall grass growing in the shallows. Every so often I saw a fish jump. A handful of fishermen were sitting at intervals along the bank, glumly watching the dark water. Their motionless lines pierced the surface like silver needles. A big white dog, apparently brought along by one of the fishermen, frisked about in the hazy spring sunshine, sniffing the clover.

When the dog reached within ten meters of where I was standing, I leaned over the fence and called out to it. The dog looked up at me with pitiful washed-out brown eyes and wagged its tail two or three times. When I snapped my fingers it came over, pushed its nose through the slats, and licked my hand with its long tongue.

"Come on, boy," I said, stepping back. The dog hesitated and looked back over its shoulder, its tail still wagging.

"Come on now—I've waited long enough."

I pulled a stick of gum from my pocket, unwrapped it, and

showed it to the dog. He stared at it for a minute before making up his mind and squeezing under the fence. I patted him on the head a few times, rolled the gum into a ball, and threw it as far as I could toward the far end of the platform. The dog made a beeline in that direction.

I went home satisfied.

Q

It's all over, I kept telling myself on the train. You can forget her now. That's why you made this trip. But I couldn't forget. That I loved Naoko. That she was dead and gone. That not a single damn thing was over and done with.

Q

The clouds that cover Venus turn its surface into a furnace. That and the humidity mean that most Venusians die young—reaching thirty brings one almost legendary status. It also means that everyone's heart is overflowing with love. Venusians all love each other; there are no exceptions. Nor is there any hatred, envy, or contempt. No one badmouths anyone else. There are no murders or fights. Love and caring reign.

"Suppose someone were to die today—we wouldn't feel sad," the quiet young Venusian said. "We loved them with all our hearts while they were alive, so there's no need for regrets."

"So you love in anticipation of death?"

"Earthling words like that escape me," he said, shaking his head.

"Do things really work out that way?" I asked.

"If they didn't," he replied, "Venus would be buried in sadness."

Ǭ

When I got back to my apartment, the twins were squeezed together in bed like sardines in a can.

"Welcome home," one of them said, giggling.

"Where have you been?" said the other, giggling too.

"At the station," I said, loosening my tie and squeezing in between them. I closed my eyes. I was dead tired.

"Which station?"

"Why did you go there?"

"A station far from here. To see a dog."

"What sort of dog?"

"You like dogs?"

"A big white dog. But no, I'm not crazy about dogs."

The two kept quiet while I smoked a cigarette.

"Sad?" one of them asked.

I nodded.

"Then sleep," said the other.

So I slept.

Ǭ

This story is about "me," but it's also about a guy they call "Rat." That autumn the two of us were living four hundred miles apart.

My novel begins in September 1973. That's the entrance. Sure hope there's an exit. Not much point in writing all this if there isn't.

ON THE BIRTH OF PINBALL

No one has a clue who Raymond Moloney was.

All we can say for sure is that a man by that name once lived and died—that's about it. Our knowledge ends there. He is as much a mystery as a water bug at the bottom of a deep well.

Yet it is a historical fact that in 1934, thanks to him, the very first pinball machine steered its way though the golden clouds of technology to safely touch down on the corrupt world below. That same year, on the other side of the big puddle of the Atlantic Ocean, Adolf Hitler grabbed the first rung of the ladder of the Weimar Republic.

Raymond Moloney's life has none of the mythical aura surrounding the lives of figures like the Wright brothers or Alexander Graham Bell. There are no heartwarming stories of childhood exploits, no dramatic eureka moments. Just one slight mention on the first page of a book written for trivia geeks: 1934—the first pinball machine, invented by Raymond Moloney. No photograph appears in the book. Needless to say, no portraits or statues were made in his honor.

I know what you're thinking. If this guy Moloney hadn't

been around, the pinball machine as we know it would be totally different. Perhaps it wouldn't even exist. Therefore our failure to appreciate him and his work smacks of ingratitude. If you could see what his invention, the Ballyhoo, looked like, however, those doubts would disappear in a flash. Nothing about it could be said to stimulate the imagination.

The pinball machine and Hitler's rise share one common trait. Greeted warily when they surfaced at that particular moment in history, their mythic aura stemmed more from the rapid pace of evolution than from any inherent quality. Evolution of the sort that moves forward on three wheels, namely Technology, Capital Investment, and Human Desire.

With terrifying speed, people seized on the crude clay doll Moloney had created and added a whole string of innovations. "Let there be light!" "Let there be electricity!" "Let there be flippers!" they cried, one after another. And so the field was illuminated, and the balls were propelled with electrically induced magnetism and directed by two armlike flippers.

A player's skill was translated into numbers and decimals, and a tilt light added to penalize anyone who nudged the table with too much enthusiasm. The metaphysical concept of "sequence" was born, which in turn spawned a host of schools: the bonus light, the extra ball, and the replay. By that time, the pinball machine had acquired an occult-like power.

Q

This is a novel about pinball.

Q

Bonus Light, a book-length study of pinball, says the following in its introduction:

Almost nothing can be gained from pinball. The only payoff is a numerical substitution for pride. The losses, however, are considerable. You could probably erect bronze statues of every American president (assuming you are willing to include Richard Nixon) with the coins you will lose, while your lost time is irreplaceable.

When you are standing before the machine engaged in your solitary act of consumption, another guy is plowing through Proust, while still another guy is doing some heavy petting with his girlfriend while watching *True Grit* at the local drive-in. They're the ones who may wind up becoming groundbreaking novelists or happily married men.

No, pinball leads nowhere. The only result is a glowing replay light. Replay, replay, replay—it makes you think the whole aim of the game is to achieve a form of eternity.

We know very little about eternity, although we can infer its existence.

The goal of pinball is self-transformation, not self-expression. It involves not the expansion of the ego but its diminution. Not analysis but all-embracing acceptance.

If it's self-expression, ego expansion, or analysis you're after, the tilt light will exact its unsparing revenge.

Have a nice game!

▸ 1

There must have been ways to tell the twin sisters apart, but I'm sad to say I never found any. Not only were their faces, voices, and hairstyles identical, they had no moles or birthmarks that might have helped me out. They were perfect copies—all I could do was throw up my hands in defeat. They responded to stimuli in precisely the same way, ate and drank the same things, sang the same songs, slept the same number of hours, had their periods at the same time.

Now, I don't know what it's like to be a twin—my powers of imagination don't extend that far. But I bet if I had a twin identical to me in every respect, it would drive me nuts. Maybe I'm a little weird that way.

The two girls, however, lived a happy and tranquil life together. They were shocked, even angry, whenever they discovered that I couldn't tell them apart.

"But we're totally different!"

"Not alike at all!"

I just shrugged.

How long had it been since they moved in? My internal clock had been off-kilter since the day we started living together. Looking back, it strikes me that my sense of time during that period had regressed to that of an organism that reproduced by cellular division.

Q

My friend and I rented a modest apartment on the street that runs up the slope from Shibuya to Nampeidai, where we opened a small translation company. We used the start-up money he got from his father, far from a princely sum, to pay the security deposit, hook up the telephone, and buy three steel desks, ten dictionaries, and half a dozen bottles of bourbon. With what was left over, we ordered a metallic signboard engraved with the company name we'd concocted, hoisted the sign out front, and placed an ad in the papers. Then we cracked open a bottle of bourbon, put our feet up on one of the desks, and waited for the customers to show up. It was the spring of 1972.

It took only a few months to realize that we had struck the mother lode. Requests poured into our humble office at an amazing clip. With the profits we bought an air conditioner, a refrigerator, and a home bar set.

"We pulled it off," said my friend. "We're successes, you and I."

That just blew me away. It was the nicest thing anyone had ever said to me.

For jobs that needed printed copies, my friend worked out an agreement with a printer he knew, even scoring a kickback on the deal. I contacted the Student Office of the University of Foreign Languages to recruit a number of bright kids to turn out rough drafts of translations, so I wouldn't get swamped. We hired a young woman to look after the books, handle the correspondence, and cover any other odd jobs that popped up. Just out of business school, she had long legs and a sharp mind. Apart from her habit of humming the melody to "Penny Lane" (minus the chorus) twenty times a day, she was perfect. We sure hit the jackpot with her, my friend said. We paid her fifty percent above the usual rate, an annual bonus equal to five months' salary, and offered a ten-day holiday in summer and then again in winter. As a result, ours was a satisfied and harmonious workplace.

Our office consisted of two rooms and an eat-in kitchen that—unusual for Tokyo—sat between the two rooms. We drew straws: I ended up with the inner room, my friend got the room next to the entranceway, and the girl sat in the kitchen, taking care of the books, fixing bourbon on the rocks, and setting out traps for the cockroaches, all to the unrelenting accompaniment of "Penny Lane."

I tapped into our expense account and bought two filing cabinets that I placed on either side of my desk, the one on the left for unfinished translations, the one on the right for those I had completed.

The manuscripts our customers brought us were a mixed bag. From an *American Science* article on ball bearings' resistance to pressure, the 1972 edition of the *All-American Book of Cocktails,* and an essay by William Styron, to a manual on the proper use and maintenance of safety razors, every item was marked "by such-and-such date" and stacked on the tray to the left, then, in due course, moved to the tray on the right. When a job was done we each drained a finger (well, a thumb, actually) of whiskey.

The great thing about doing translations at our level was that it didn't require any extra thought. You simply took a coin (the original text) in your left hand, plunked it on your right palm, whisked your left hand away, and there it was. Simple.

We arrived at the office at ten and left at four. On Saturdays the three of us went to a nearby disco, where we drank J&B and danced to a Santana cover band.

The money wasn't bad. From our monthly earnings we subtracted the rent, a small amount for office expenses, pay for our secretary and the part-timers, and taxes, then divided the remainder into ten parts, of which one part went to our business savings account, five parts to him, and four parts to me. To divvy up the money we piled it all on the table in cash and worked from there, like the poker scene between Steve

McQueen and Edward G. Robinson in *The Cincinnati Kid*. Primitive, for sure, but a heck of a lot of fun.

I think it made sense that my friend got five parts to my four. Not only did I foist the entire business side of our operation onto him, he endured the times I overdid the whiskey without complaint. On top of that, he had a sick wife, a three-year-old son, a Volkswagen Beetle with a wonky radiator, and, as if all that weren't enough, a compulsion to take on even more headaches.

"I'm looking after twin girls myself," I told him once, but of course he didn't buy it. So he kept on getting five to my four.

I spent my mid-twenties like this. Days as peaceful as a pool of afternoon sunlight.

The company slogan we stuck on our tri-colored promotional brochure read, "What the human hand can write, we can translate."

When, every six months or so, our business went into a rare slump, the three of us killed time handing those brochures out in front of Shibuya Station.

How long did things go on like that? I walked on and on through a boundless silence. I went home every day after work to read the *Critique of Pure Reason* yet again and drink the twins' delicious coffee.

Sometimes things that happened the day before felt like they had occurred a year earlier; at other times last year's events seemed to have happened yesterday. When it got really bad, next year's events seemed to have taken place the previous day. Sometimes I found myself ruminating on ball bearings while translating Kenneth Tynan's article on Roman Polanski from the September 1971 issue of *Esquire*.

Month after month, year after year, I sat alone at the bottom of a deep swimming pool. Warm water, gentle light, and silence. Then, more silence . . .

Q

There was just one way for me to tell the twins apart. That was by their sweatshirts. Each wore a faded navy-blue sweatshirt with white numerals printed on the chest. One read "208," the other "209." The "2" fit squarely on top of the right nipple, the "8" (or "9") atop the left nipple. The "0" was plunked smack in the middle.

The very first day I had asked them what the numbers meant. Nothing at all, came the response.

"They look like serial numbers," I said, using the English word.

"What are those?" one asked.

"Like if a whole bunch of you were manufactured at the same time, and you were each given a number."

"No way," said 208.

"Yeah," said 209. "There've been just the two of us from the start. And somebody gave us these shirts, anyway."

"Who?"

"We got them at the supermarket. It was their opening day, and a whole bunch of us got them for free."

"I was the 209th customer," said 209.

"And I was the 208th," said 208.

"We bought three boxes of tissues."

"Okay, so let's do it this way: I'll call you 208. And you 209,"

I said, pointing to each of them in turn. "That way I can tell you apart."

"Won't work," said one.

"Why not?"

They pulled off their sweatshirts, exchanged them, and pulled them on again.

"Now I'm 208," said 209.

"And I'm 209," said 208.

I let out a sigh.

Still, whenever I had to distinguish between the two of them, I relied on the numbers on their sweatshirts. There was just no other way to tell who was who.

They had arrived with only the clothes on their backs. It was as if they had been taking a stroll, seen a promising place, and moved in. Well, I guess that's about how it happened. I gave them some money at the beginning of each week to buy what they needed, but apart from food for our meals, the only thing they ever purchased was an occasional box of coffee cream cookies.

"Isn't it a problem, not having more clothes?" I asked.

"No problem at all," replied 208.

"We don't care about clothes," answered 209.

They tenderly laundered their sweatshirts once a week in the bath. Lying in bed reading the *Critique of Pure Reason*, I would glance up and see them kneeling side by side, naked on the tile floor, scrubbing away. Times like that made me feel as if I'd arrived at some faraway place. Why, I don't know. I'd been experiencing the same feeling from time to time since the previous summer, when I had lost the crown from my front tooth under the diving board at the pool.

Many times I came home after work to see the sweatshirts with the numbers 208 and 209 fluttering in my south-facing window. Occasionally it brought tears to my eyes.

Ǫ

There were so many questions I could have asked. Why did you choose my place? How long will you stay? Most of all, what are you? How old are you? Where were you born? But I never asked, and they never said.

We spent our mornings drinking coffee, our evenings trolling the golf course for lost balls, and our nights fooling around in bed. The highlight was the hour or so I spent each day explaining items in the newspaper. They knew so little about the world. I mean, they couldn't tell the difference between Burma and Australia. It took three days to get across the fact that Vietnam had been divided into two sides that were now at war, and four to explain why Nixon had decided to bomb Hanoi.

"So which are you rooting for?" asked 208.

"Which?"

"The north or the south?" said 209.

"I don't know. That's a hard one."

"Why is it so hard?" That was 208.

"Because I don't live in Vietnam."

That didn't convince them. It didn't convince me either.

"So why are they fighting? Political differences, right?" 208 grilled me.

"I guess you could say that."

"So their ideas are in conflict?" continued 208.

"Yes. But then you could say that there are 1.2 million conflicting ideas in the world. Probably more."

"So then it's almost impossible to be friends with anyone?" That was 209.

"That's true," I said. "It's just about impossible to be friends."

This was my lifestyle in the 1970s. Prophesied by Dostoevsky, consolidated by yours truly.

▸ **2**

In the autumn of 1973, we could sense something nasty lurking just out of sight. The Rat felt it like a pebble in his shoe.

The brief summer had been sent on its way by the shifting winds of early September; yet the Rat seemed lost in what few traces remained. Still wearing his old T-shirt, cutoff jeans, and sandals, he made the daily commute to J's Bar, where he sat at the counter talking to J the bartender and drinking over-chilled beer. He had quit cigarettes five years before, but now he was smoking again and checking his watch every fifteen minutes.

It appeared as though time had stopped for the Rat, as if all of a sudden its flow had been severed. The Rat had no idea why things had changed. Nor did he know how to search for the severed end. He could only wander through the autumn gloom with a limp piece of rope in his hand. He crossed meadows, forded rivers, pushed open doors. But the rope led him nowhere. He was as powerless and lonely as a winter fly stripped of its wings, or a river confronting the sea. An ill wind had arisen somewhere, and it was blowing the warm, familiar air that had embraced him to the other side of the planet.

One season had opened the door and left, while another

had entered through a second door. You might run to the open door and call out, Wait, there's something I forgot to tell you! But no one is there. When you close the door, you turn around to see the new season sitting in a chair, lighting up a cigarette. If you forgot to tell him something, he says, then why not tell me? I might pass the message along if I get the chance. No, that's all right, you say. It's no big deal. The sound of wind fills the room. No big deal. Just another season dead and gone.

Q

The rich university dropout and the solitary Chinese bartender sat shoulder to shoulder, like an old married couple, as autumn once again gave way to the chill of winter.

Autumn was always a real downer. The few friends who had returned to town during summer vacation had already said their quick goodbyes and headed back to their distant new homes without waiting for September's arrival. As if crossing an invisible watershed, the summer light began its imperceptible change and the brilliant aura that had filled the Rat's world during that brief span vanished. Like a creek flowing onto autumn's sandy soil, the remnants of his warm summer dreams were sucked away without a trace.

Autumn was no fun for J either. When mid-September came, the number of his customers plummeted. It was like that every year, but this time around the drop-off was shocking. Neither J nor the Rat could understand what was behind the change. All they could know was that the bucket of potatoes J had peeled for frying was still half full when closing time came.

"Just wait," the Rat consoled him. "Pretty soon you'll be bitching about how busy it is."

"I wonder," J said, looking unconvinced. He sat down on the stool behind the counter and started chipping burned butterfat off the toaster oven with an ice pick.

No one knew what might be waiting around the corner.

While the Rat leafed through a book, J ran a dry cloth over the bottles on the shelves, pausing to drag on the unfiltered cigarette clamped between his callused fingers.

Ｑ

The Rat's sense of time had begun to go haywire three years earlier. The same spring that he quit the university.

There were, of course, a number of reasons why he had left school. These were all entangled with each other, and when they heated up, the fuse blew with a bang. Some things were left unchanged, some were blown away to parts unknown, some died.

The Rat did not try to explain why he had quit. A proper explanation could have taken a good five hours. Besides, if he explained himself to one person, soon everyone else he knew might demand to hear his story. From there it was a small step to having to explain himself to the whole world. Just imagining that made the Rat sick to his stomach.

"I didn't like the way they cut the grass in the school quad," he would say when pressed.

One girl actually went to the quad to check. "Didn't look that bad to me," she said. "Though there was some trash strewn around . . ."

"It's a matter of taste," the Rat replied.

When the Rat was in a better mood, he let on a bit more. "We just didn't get along," he would say, "me and school." Then he would clam up.

This was three years ago.

But everything had passed with the flow of time. At an almost unbelievable pace. What had once been a violent, panting flood of emotion had suddenly withdrawn, leaving behind a heap of what felt like meaningless old dreams.

The Rat had left home the year he entered university and moved into an apartment his father had once used as a study. His parents voiced no objections to the move. They had planned to give the place to their son at some point anyway, and figured it wouldn't be a bad thing for him to experience the hardship of living on his own for a while.

Whatever way one looked at it, though, his life there could hardly be seen as difficult. No more than a melon could be mistaken for a vegetable. The apartment was beautifully designed and boasted three comfortable rooms, an air conditioner and a phone, a seventeen-inch color television set, a bath and a shower, a Mercedes Triumph in the underground parking lot, and, to top it all off, a fancy balcony perfect for sunbathing. The southeast-facing window of the penthouse afforded a panoramic view of town and ocean. When the Rat opened both windows, the chirping of birds and the heady fragrance of trees wafted in on the wind.

The Rat spent many tranquil afternoons settled in his rattan chair. When he began to drift off, he could feel time pass through his body like gently flowing water. As he sat, hours, days, weeks went by.

Occasionally, ripples of emotion would lap against his heart as if to remind him of something. When that happened, he closed his eyes, clamped his heart shut, and waited for the emotions to recede. It was only a brief sensation, like the shadows that signal the coming of night. Once the ripples had passed, the quiet calm returned as if nothing untoward had ever taken place.

▸ **3**

Unless you count people peddling newspaper subscriptions, no one ever knocks at my door. So it stays shut, and I never have to answer to anyone.

That Sunday morning, though, whoever it was knocked thirty-five times. What could I do? With my eyes half closed, I dragged myself out of bed and stumbled to the door. A man of about forty in a gray workman's uniform was standing there in the hall, cradling his helmet like a small puppy.

"I'm from the phone company," he said. "I've come to replace your switch panel."

I nodded, leaning against the door frame. The guy's face was black with stubble, the kind of beard you could shave over and over without ever getting rid of it all. He even had hair growing under his eyes. I felt sorry for him, but I was zonked out. The twins and I had been playing backgammon until four in the morning.

"Can't we make it this afternoon?"

"No, I'm afraid it has to be now."

"Why?"

The man fumbled in the outside pocket of his work pants before extracting a black notebook. "Look," he said, showing it to me. "This is my schedule for today. After I finish here, I have to head to another part of the city. See?"

I looked at the notebook from where I stood. It was upside down, but I was able to see that, sure enough, my apartment was his last call in this neighborhood.

"What do you have to do?"

"It's simple. I pull out the old switch panel, cut the wires, and hook up the new one. That's all. The whole thing takes about ten minutes."

I thought for a moment before shaking my head no.

"I'm happy with the one I've got," I said.

"But it's an old model."

"The old model's fine with me."

He thought for a moment. "It's like this," he said at last. "This isn't just about you. It affects everyone."

"How so?"

"The switch panels are all hooked up to the central computer at headquarters. So if yours is sending out a different signal than the rest, we've got a big problem. Got it?"

"Yes, I get it. You're talking about matching up hardware and software."

"Then can't you see your way to letting me in?"

What could I do? I opened the door and ushered him inside.

"But why would my apartment have the switch panel?" I asked. "Wouldn't it go in the super's apartment, or someplace like that?"

"*Normally,*" he said, scanning the walls of my kitchen. "But switch panels are just big nuisances to most people. They take up a lot of space, after all, and they're hardly ever used."

I nodded. Now the guy had climbed up on one of my kitchen

chairs in his socks and was checking the ceiling. Nothing there, either.

"It's like a treasure hunt. People cram switch panels into the weirdest places. It's a real pity. Then they decorate their apartments with bulky doll cases and monster pianos. Go figure."

I agreed. Giving up on the kitchen, he opened the bedroom door, still shaking his head.

"Let me tell you about a switch panel I came across the other day. Where do you think they tossed the poor thing? Couldn't believe my eyes . . ."

He caught his breath. With the covers pulled to their chins, the twins lay side by side—with space for me in the middle—in a huge bed in a corner of the room. For fifteen seconds the repairman stood there dumbfounded. The twins were silent too. I had no choice but to break the ice.

"Uh, this gentleman is here with the phone company."

"Hi," said the one on the right.

"Welcome," said the one on the left.

"How . . . how do you do," said the repairman.

"He's come to replace the switch panel," I said.

"The switch panel?"

"What's that?"

"It's a machine to control the circuits."

Neither of them understood. So I stepped back and let the repairman take over.

"Hmm . . . You see, it's where all the telephone circuits gather together. Kind of like a mother dog with lots of puppies. Get it?"

"?"

"Nope."

"Okay, so let's say this mother dog is raising her puppies . . . But if she dies, then her puppies will all die too. So when her time comes, we go around replacing her with a new mother."

"Cool."

"Amazing."

I had to hand it to him.

"So that's why I'm here. Awful sorry to come at such a bad time."

"No problem."

"I want to watch."

The relieved repairman mopped his brow with his handkerchief.

"Now if I can find the panel," he said, scanning the room.

"No need to search," said the one on the right.

"It's in the closet," said the one on the left. "Just remove the boards."

I was blown away. "How come you guys know? Even *I* didn't know that."

"It's the switch panel, right?"

"It's famous."

"I'm floored," said the repairman.

The job took ten minutes, and the whole time the twins had their heads together, giggling about something. As a result, the repairman kept botching the hookup. When he finally finished, the twins wriggled into their jeans and sweatshirts under the sheets and bounced into the kitchen to make coffee for everyone.

I offered the repairman a leftover Danish to go with his coffee. He jumped at the chance.

"Thanks so much. I missed breakfast."

"Don't you have a wife?" asked 208.

"Sure I do. But she sleeps in on Sundays."

"Poor guy," said 209.

"It's not like I choose to work Sundays, either."

I felt sorry for him. "How about a boiled egg?" I asked.

"That would be an imposition."

"No problem," I said. "We're all having some."

"Well, in that case. Not too runny, though . . ."

$\bigcirc$

"I've been making house calls for twenty-one years," the repairman said as he peeled his egg, "but I've never seen anything like this before."

"Anything like what?" I asked.

"Well, uh . . . you're sleeping with twins, right? Doesn't that wear you out?"

"No," I said, sipping my coffee.

"Really?"

"Really."

"He's something else," said 208.

"Yeah," said 209. "A real animal."

"I'm floored," said the man.

$\bigcirc$

I think he really was floored. The giveaway was that he forgot to take the old switch panel when he departed. Or maybe he left it behind to thank us for the breakfast. At any rate, the twins played with it all day, one acting as the mother dog, the other as the puppies. I couldn't make heads or tails of what they were talking about.

So I put them out of my mind and spent the afternoon focused on the translation I had brought home. The student part-timers who did the rough drafts were taking their exams, so my work had piled up. I was flying along until about three o'clock, when my battery began to run down and my pace slowed; by four the battery was dead. I couldn't write another line.

I planted my elbows on the glass desktop, lit up a cigarette, and gazed at the ceiling. The smoke looked like ectoplasm as it wandered through the quiet afternoon light. September 1973— it felt like a dream. Did 1973 *really* exist? I had never thought about it before. Somehow the idea struck me as hilarious.

"Are you okay?" asked 208.

"Just tired. Feel like some coffee?"

They trooped off to the kitchen, where one ground the beans and the other boiled the water and warmed the cups. Then we plopped down in a row on the floor next to the window and drank our coffee.

"Not going so great?" asked 209.

"I've had better days," I answered.

"It's in bad shape," said 208.

"What is?"

"The switch panel."

"The mother dog."

I let out a very deep sigh. "You think so?"

They both nodded.

"It's dying."

"For real."

"So what should we do?"

"We don't know," they said, shaking their heads.

I puffed on my cigarette. "How about if we take a stroll around the golf course?" I said a little while later. "It's Sunday, so there could be tons of lost balls."

After about an hour of backgammon, we scaled the chain-link fence and walked the deserted course in the twilight. I whistled the tune to Mildred Bailey's "It's So Peaceful in the Country" twice. The twins said they liked the song a lot. But we didn't find a single golf ball. Sometimes it's like that. Every low-handicap golfer in Tokyo must have played there that day. Or maybe they had brought in a specially trained beagle to retrieve lost balls. Feeling low, we trudged back to the apartment.

▶ 4

The unmanned beacon sat alone at the end of a long, meandering pier. It was not particularly big, a little less than ten feet tall. Fishing boats had relied on its light in the days before pollution drove the fish from the coast. There was nothing resembling a harbor in the area. Instead, the fishermen had rigged a set of wooden tracks with a winch and a rope to pull their boats up from the beach. Three of their huts had stood nearby; in the mornings you would have seen wooden boxes of small fish drying inside the breakwater. At a certain point, however, the fishermen had left, driven away by a combination of three factors: the disappearance of the fish, the commuters' irrational aversion to having a fishing village near their town, and the township's declaration that the huts along the beach were illegal. That was 1962. Where the fishermen had gone was anyone's guess. The three houses were summarily demolished, while the rotting boats, with no further function and no place to be discarded, were left high and dry among the trees along the shore, where they served as a playground for children.

Once the fishing boats were gone, private yachts wandering the coast and freighters moored outside the port seeking shelter from typhoons and heavy fogs were the only vessels left that might have found the beacon helpful. But most likely it no longer served a purpose.

The beacon was a squat black thing shaped like a bell set down on its rim or a man hunched in thought seen from the back. When the sun began to set and the evening glow became tinged with blue, an orange light glowed from its top—the handle of the bell—and it slowly began to revolve. In that instant, when day turned to night, it came to life: whether evening brought a beautiful sunset or a cloak of mist, the beam began to rotate at the precise moment when the balance between light and dark shifted, and darkness reigned supreme.

As a child, the Rat had often gone down to the beach in the evenings just to witness that sudden flash in the dark. If the waves were not too high he would walk to the end of the twisting pier, counting its worn flagstones as he went. In the early fall he could see schools of tiny fish darting about in the surprisingly clear water. They would swim circles along the sides of the pier, as if searching for something, before heading out to sea.

When at last he reached the beacon, the Rat sat down on the end of the pier and studied the sky. It was dark blue as far as the eye could see, with streaks of cloud that looked painted by an artist's brush. The blue seemed bottomless; its depth made the

Rat's legs tremble in awe. Everything was so vivid, the smell of the ocean, the color of the wind. Taking his time, the Rat drank in the scene that lay before him, then turned around. Now he was looking at his own world, so separate from the deep sea. The white beach and the breakwater, the flattened row of green pines, and, behind them, ranged against the sky, the sharp outline of the bluish-black mountains.

Far to his left was the great port, with its cranes, floating docks, boxlike warehouses, freighters, and tall buildings. To his right, facing the ocean and running along the curved coastline, were the quiet residential district, the yacht harbor, some old sake warehouses, and, a suitable distance beyond, the industrial zone's row of spherical tanks and towering smokestacks, which covered the sky with a white haze. That marked the end of the world as the ten-year-old Rat knew it.

Throughout his childhood, from spring to early autumn, the Rat paid regular visits to the beacon. When the waves were high, the spray washed his feet, the wind howled, and he slipped time and again on the mossy flagstones. Yet the path to the beacon was dearer to him than anywhere else. He would sit there at the end of the pier listening to the waves, gazing at the clouds, the sky, and the schools of small fish, and tossing the pebbles he carried in his pocket into the water.

When the sky darkened he would take the same path back to his own world. This return, though, was always accompanied by an ineffable sadness. The world awaiting him out there was just too big, too powerful; there seemed to be no place where he could burrow into it.

.   .   .

The woman's apartment was not far from the pier. Vague memories of his childhood and the smell of those evenings came back to the Rat each time he visited her. He would park on the coastal road and cut through the sparse stand of pine trees planted to block the sand blowing in from the beach. The sand made a dry sound under his feet.

The apartment building was located where the fishermen's huts had once stood. If you dug down a few meters, reddish-brown seawater came bubbling up. South American canna lilies drooped in the front garden, as if someone had trampled them. The woman lived on the second floor—when the wind blew it brushed her window with fine sand. Her neat little apartment faced south, but it was strangely gloomy. It's the ocean, she said. It's too damn close—the smell of the tide, the wind, the sound of the waves, the stink of fish . . . everything.

"You can't smell fish here," the Rat said.

Sure I can, she said. She pulled a cord and the Venetian blinds closed with a snap. So would you if you lived here.

Sand swept against the window.

▸ 5

When I was in college, no one in my apartment building had a phone. Hell, I doubt any of us had an eraser. There was, though, one pink pay phone, which sat outside the caretaker's office on a low table that had been tossed out by the local elementary school. It was the only phone in the whole place. Telephone switch panels were the last thing on our minds. Ours was a peaceful world in a peaceful time.

Since the caretaker was never in his office, one of us had to answer the phone when it rang and dash off to inform the recipient of their call. Of course there were times (like when a call came in at 2 a.m.) when no one picked up. Like an elephant aware of its approaching death, the phone would ring like mad (the most I counted was thirty-two times) and then die. I use the word die literally. The moment the last ring had sailed down the long corridor and off into the black night, a hush settled over the building. It was an eerie silence. We all lay there in our beds, holding our breath, as we contemplated the dead call.

Late-night calls were always depressing. Someone would pick up the receiver and start talking in a low voice:

"Let's drop it . . . No, you've got it wrong . . . What's done is done, right? . . . It's the truth. Why would I lie? . . . No, I'm just tired . . . Of course it bothers me . . . But you see . . . Yeah, I get the picture. But I need time, okay? . . . I can't explain over the phone . . ."

Each of us had all the troubles we could carry. They rained down on us from the sky, and we raced around in a frenzy to pick them up and stuff them in our pockets. Why we did that stumps me, even now. Maybe we thought they were something else.

There were telegrams, too. A motorbike would roar up to the front door around four in the morning, followed by loud footsteps in the hallway. Then a fist would pound on some-one's door. That noise always reminded me of the Grim Reaper. Boom, boom. We were prone to so many disasters—lives lost to suicide, minds wrecked, hearts marooned in the backwaters of time, bodies burning with pointless obsessions—and we gave each other a hell of a lot of trouble. Nineteen seventy was that kind of year. Yet if you cling to the belief that the human organism is made to improve itself through some sort of dialectical process, a year as awful as 1970 can teach you something.

Q

My room was on the first floor next to the caretaker's office, while the girl with the long hair lived on the second floor, next to the stairs. Since she was the clear winner when it came to the number of calls received, I was stuck trotting up and down those fifteen slippery steps thousands of times to summon her to the phone. Her callers were all sorts of people. Their voices were courteous or officious, sad or arrogant. In all cases they asked for her by name. Yet I have no memory of what that name was. My only recollection is that it was heartbreakingly common.

Her voice on the phone was an almost inaudible, exhausted-sounding whisper. Her face was attractive enough, but kind of gloomy. Although we passed each other on the street from time to time, I never spoke to her. Her expression as she walked along was like that of someone riding a white elephant down a narrow jungle path.

Q

She lived in our apartment building for six months. From the beginning of autumn to the end of winter.

I would answer the phone, climb the stairs, knock on her door, say, "Phone for you," and a moment later she would say, "Thanks." "Thanks" was all she ever said to me. Then again, "Phone for you" was all I ever said to her.

It was a lonely season for me as well. When I returned to my room and undressed at the end of the day, my bones threatened to burst through my skin and fly away. As if some mysterious internal force were propelling me in the wrong direction, leading me toward another world.

The phone calls made me think. Someone was trying to get through to someone else. Yet almost no one ever called me. Not a single person was trying to reach me, and even if they had been, they wouldn't have said what I wanted to hear.

Each of us had, to a greater or lesser degree, resolved to live according to his or her own system. If another person's way of thinking was too different from mine, it made me mad; too close, and I got sad. That's all there was to it.

Ǫ

It was the end of winter when I fielded her last phone call. A clear Saturday morning in early March. Mid-morning anyway, ten o'clock, with bright winter sunlight probing every corner of my small room. When I became aware of the ringing, I was sitting on my bed looking out the window at the cabbage field next door. Glistening patches of snow were scattered across the black soil like puddles of water—all that remained of the last snow of the final cold snap of the year.

The phone rang ten times without anyone picking up. Then five minutes later it started again. That ticked me off, but I threw a cardigan over my pajamas and went to get it.

"Is Miss . . . there?" asked a man. His voice was flat, elusive. Mumbling something noncommittal, I trudged up the stairs and knocked on her door.

"Phone for you."

"Thanks."

I went back to my room, lay down on the bed, and studied the ceiling. I could hear her coming down the steps, and then that whispery voice. It was an unusually short conversation for her. Maybe fifteen seconds. I heard her hang up and then there was a protracted silence, no footsteps, nothing. A moment later, I heard footsteps slowly approaching my door, followed by two knocks. There was a pause for as long as a deep breath, then another two raps.

When I opened the door she was standing there in a bulky white sweater and jeans. I thought for a moment I had made a mistake, that the call had been for someone else, but she said nothing, just stood there shivering with her arms folded and her eyes fixed on me. She looked like someone in a lifeboat watching the ship go down. Or maybe the other way around.

"Can I come in? It's freezing out here."

I was taken off guard, but I let her in and closed the door. She sat down in front of my gas heater to warm her hands and looked around.

"This room is awfully bare, isn't it?"

I nodded. There really was nothing. Just a bed next to a window, and that was it. A bed too big for one, and too small for two. I hadn't bought it. Rather, an acquaintance had given it to me. Why he had given it to a virtual stranger was beyond me. We seldom talked. A rich kid from the middle of nowhere, he had quit school after he was beaten by members of an opposing political group who kicked him in the head with their construction boots, damaging his eyesight. It had happened in the quad, and he had sobbed all the way from there to the school infirmary, to my great disgust. A few days later he told me he was leaving school. And gave me the bed.

"Is there anything warm to drink?" she said. No, I answered, shaking my head. No coffee, no tea, not even a proper kettle. Just a saucepan to boil water in the morning when I shaved. Wait here, she said with a sigh. She stood up and left the room, returning five minutes later with a cardboard box in her hands. Inside was a good six months' supply of tea bags and green tea, two bags of cookies, granulated sugar, a basic set of pots and plates, and two Snoopy glasses. Setting the box down on the bed, she pulled out a pot and began to boil water.

"How do you get by? You live like Robinson Crusoe!"

"It's not that much fun."

"I guess not."

We drank our black tea in silence.

"You can have all this," she said.

I choked on my tea. "Why would you do that?"

"It's my way of saying thanks. For all the times you answered the phone."

"But won't you need it?"

She shook her head. "I'm moving out tomorrow. It's of no use to me anymore."

There must have been something to explain this new train of events, but I couldn't imagine what.

"Did something good happen? Or was it something bad?"

"Not too good, I guess. I mean I'm dropping out of school and going home."

The winter sunlight that filled the room dimmed for a moment, then brightened again.

"But you don't want to hear about it, do you? I sure wouldn't. Who'd want to use the dishes of someone who'd bummed them out!"

.　　.　　.

The next morning, a cold rain began to fall. It was a fine rain that managed to seep through my raincoat and soak the sweater beneath. Everything—the big trunk I was lugging and the suitcase and shoulder bag she carried—was dark with moisture. The taxi driver snapped at us not to put any of it on the seat. The cab was hot and stuffy with stale tobacco smoke, and a traditional ballad was blaring from the car radio, a tune as old-fashioned as a semaphore indicator. The dripping branches of the leafless trees lining both sides of the road looked like underwater coral.

"I didn't like Tokyo the first time I laid eyes on it," she said, "and I still don't."

"Really?"

"Yes. The soil is too black, the rivers are filthy, there aren't any mountains . . . How about you?"

"I've never thought about the scenery."

She sighed. "That's why you're going to survive this place," she said with a smile.

We reached the platform and put down the bags.

"Thanks for everything," she said. "I can take it from here."

"Where's home?"

"Way up north."

"I bet it's cold."

"That's okay. I'm used to it."

When the train started moving she waved to me from the window. I raised my hand to the level of my ear, but when the train went out of sight, I felt awkward all of a sudden and stuffed it in the pocket of my raincoat.

It rained all day and on into the night. I bought two bottles of beer at the local liquor store and drank them in one of the glasses she had given me. I was freezing cold. The glass had a picture of Snoopy and Woodstock playing on top of Snoopy's doghouse with a balloon that read, "Happiness is a warm friend."

The twins were fast asleep when I opened my eyes. Three a.m. The autumn moonlight outside the bathroom window was unnaturally bright. I sat on the edge of the kitchen counter next to the sink, drank two glasses of water, and lit a cigarette on the gas burner. The layered voices of thousands upon thousands of insects rose from the moonlit golf course.

I picked up the switch panel leaning against the counter and examined it with care, turning it this way and that. It was just a meaningless board, grimy and old, no matter how you looked at it. Giving up, I put it back where it had been, wiped the dirt from my hands, and took another puff on my cigarette. Everything looked pale in the moonlight. Devoid of value, meaning, or direction. Even the shadows were indistinct. I stubbed out my cigarette in the sink and lit another.

Would I ever find a place that was truly mine? Where might it be? I thought and thought, yet all that came to me was the cockpit of a twin-seater torpedo plane. But that was sheer idiocy. I mean, those things went out of date thirty years ago, right?

I went back to bed and squeezed in between the twins. They lay curled with their heads angled toward the outer edges of the bed, breathing peacefully. I pulled the blanket to my chin and studied the ceiling.

▶ **6**

The woman stepped into the bathroom and closed the door behind her. The sound of the shower followed soon after.

The Rat struggled to control his feelings. He raised himself on the sheets, grabbed a cigarette, and put it between his lips. But his lighter wasn't on the table or in the pocket of his trousers. He didn't even have a match. He poked around in the woman's bag, but no luck there either. Giving up, he switched on the light and rifled through his desk drawers until he turned up an old book of matches with the name of some restaurant on it. He lit his cigarette.

Her stockings and underwear were folded with care and piled on one of his rattan chairs, her tailored mustard-colored dress draped over its back. On the bedside table lay her tiny watch and her La Bagagerie bag, no longer new but well maintained.

The Rat sank down in the opposite chair and stared out the window.

From his mountainside perch, the Rat could see the signs of human activity scattered across the hillside below. Sometimes he stood there for hours, hands on hips, focusing on the scene below like a golfer at the top of a downhill course. The slope descended at a gentle angle, gathering in the scattered lights of the houses. There were dark groves of trees, small hills, and, here and there, private swimming pools glaring white under mercury lamps. Where the slope began to level off, the highway snaked across the landscape like an illuminated waistband; from the base of the mountain to the shore half a mile away, the town sprawled flat and monotonous. The ocean beyond melted into the dark sky, while the orange light from the small beacon flashed, disappeared, and flashed again. And cutting through all these layers of terrain, dividing them neatly in two, ran the dark fairway.

The river.

◯

The Rat had first met the woman in early September, when the sky still retained a trace of summer radiance.

He had found an electric typewriter listed in the Used Goods section of his local newspaper among ads for playpens, Linguaphones, tricycles, and whatnot. The young woman who answered the phone sounded very businesslike: the typewriter had been used for a year with a year left on its warranty; cash up front (no monthly payments); he had to come get it himself. They struck a deal, and he drove to her apartment, paid, and picked up the typewriter. It cost nearly as much as what he had earned from his part-time summer job.

She was small and slender and wore an attractive sleeveless dress. Leafy plants of various shapes and colors were lined up in pots at the apartment's entranceway. She had pleasant features, and her hair was tied up at the back. The Rat couldn't tell her age. He would have found anything between twenty-two and twenty-eight believable.

Three days later, she phoned to say that she had half a dozen typewriter ribbons she would be happy to give him for free. When the Rat picked them up, he asked her out to J's Bar, where he treated her to cocktails to thank her for the ribbons. They didn't click right off the bat, though.

The third time they met was four days later, at the local indoor pool. He drove her back to his apartment and they made love. Why did it turn out that way? The Rat had no idea. Did he make the first move or did she? They had simply gone with the flow.

After a few days, the Rat could feel the tangible reality of their relationship swelling within him, as if a soft wedge were being driven into his everyday life. Little by little, something was getting through. His long-forgotten gentler, sweeter side seemed to expand each time he thought of her slender arms wrapped around his body.

The Rat could see that she was trying to establish a kind of perfection in her small world. He was well aware that required an extraordinary degree of determination. She wore only the most modest yet tasteful dresses over fresh, clean undergarments, applied an eau de cologne with the fragrance of a morning vineyard to her body, took great care in choosing her words, asked no pointless questions, and appeared to have practiced smiling in the mirror. Yet these things only added to the Rat's sadness. After a number of meetings he guessed her age to be twenty-seven. That turned out to be spot on.

Her breasts were small, and though her trim body was beautifully tanned, it was a reluctant rather than a boastful tan, as if it had been acquired without her approval. Her angular cheekbones and thin lips spoke of her good upbringing and resolute core, but there was something naive and vulnerable beneath the surface, which showed in her subtle shifts of expression.

She had studied architecture in an art college, she said, and now worked in an architect's office. Her birthplace? Nowhere near here, she replied. I came to this area after I graduated. She went to the pool once a week and took the train to her viola lesson every Sunday night.

The two of them got together once a week, on Saturday night. Then the Rat spent Sunday in a haze while she practiced playing Mozart.

▸ **7**

I missed three whole days of work with a cold, and when I got back, I was swamped. My mouth was gritty, and my body felt as if it had been scrubbed with sandpaper. Piles of documents—pamphlets, manuscripts, booklets, magazines, etc.—rose like anthills around my desk. My business partner stopped by to mumble a few words of what sounded like sympathy and went back to his room. The girl left the usual coffee and two rolls on my desk, then she disappeared as well. I had forgotten to buy cigarettes, so I bummed a pack of Seven Stars from·my partner, popped the filter off one, turned it around, and lit it. The sky outside was gray and hazy—you couldn't tell where the air ended and the clouds began. The smell of smoke was in the air, as if someone were trying to burn wet leaves. But that may have been my fever.

I took a deep breath and set to work on the anthill closest to me. Everything in it was stamped Urgent, with the deadline written below in red felt pen. Luckily, it was the only anthill marked Urgent. Even luckier, none of the documents was so urgent it had to be completed in the next two or three days. All the deadlines were one or two weeks away, so chances were I could get everything done in time if I sent half out to our part-timers for rough translation. I picked up the documents one by one and arranged them in the order I would work on them. This made the anthill much less stable than before: now it was shaped like a newspaper graph indicating the Cabinet's approval rating by gender and age. The mix of topics, though, really turned me on.

① **AUTHOR**: CHARLES RANKIN
  TITLE: *Readers' Questions on Science (Animals)*
  LENGTH: *From p. 68 ("Why does a cat wash its face?")*
    to p. 89 ("How does a bear catch fish?")
  DUE: *October 12*

② **AUTHOR**: THE AMERICAN NURSING ASSOCIATION
  TITLE: *Conversing with the Terminally Ill*
  LENGTH: *16 pages*
  DUE: *October 19*

③ **AUTHOR**: FRANK DESITO JR.
  TITLE: *A Study of Writers' Pathology, Chapter Three:*
    "Writers on Hay Fever"
  LENGTH: *23 pages*
  DUE: *October 23*

④ **AUTHOR**: RENÉ CLAIR
  TITLE: *The Italian Straw Hat (English translation of the film*
    script)
  LENGTH: *39 pages*
  DUE: *October 26*

Too bad the clients' names weren't included! Who had commissioned these translations (and "urgently," no less), and for what reasons? I hadn't a clue. Was there a bear patiently standing beside a river somewhere waiting for my translation to arrive? Or a tongue-tied nurse unable to speak a word to her dying patient?

Tossing the photograph of a cat washing its face with one paw on the desk, I drank my coffee and ate one of the rolls, which tasted like plaster of Paris. My head was starting to clear, but the fever was causing some numbness in my fingertips and toes. I reached into my desk drawer for my Swiss Army knife, selected six HB pencils, and took my time sharpening them to a fine point as I eased into work.

My cassette tape of an old Stan Getz album was the musical background for my efforts that morning. It was a dynamite band featuring Getz, Al Haig, Jimmy Raney, Teddy Kotick, and Tiny Kahn. Whistling Getz's solo to "Jumpin' with Symphony Sid" from start to finish along with the tape really picked me up.

I broke at noon for a lunch of fried fish at a crowded restaurant five minutes' walk down the slope and followed that with two quick shots of orange juice at a hamburger stand. From there I continued on to a pet shop, where I spent ten minutes playing with an Abyssinian cat, poking my finger through an opening in the front window. A typical lunch break.

I went back to my office and leafed through the morning paper until the hands on the clock pointed to one. I sharpened six more pencils for my afternoon's work and pinched the filters off the rest of the pack of Seven Stars, lining the cigarettes up on my desk. The girl brought in a hot cup of green tea.

"How do you feel?"

"Not so bad."

"How's the work going?"

"Couldn't be better."

Outside it was still overcast. In fact the gray seemed only to have deepened since morning. When I stuck my head out the window I thought I sniffed rain. A few autumn birds cut across the sky. The drone of the city was everywhere, a mix of countless sounds: subway trains, sizzling hamburgers, cars on elevated highways, automatic doors opening and closing.

Shutting the window, I put on a tape of Charlie Parker's "Just Friends" and dug into the next translation, "When Do Migrating Birds Sleep?"

I wrapped up work at four, gave what I had translated to the girl, and headed out. Instead of lugging an umbrella, I wore the thin raincoat I kept in the office for times like this. I bought an evening paper at the station and spent the next hour being tossed around in the packed train. I could smell rain there too, although a single drop had yet to fall.

I had just finished shopping for dinner at the supermarket in front of the station when the rain began. The drops were too fine to see, but the sidewalk at my feet was turning a darker shade of gray. I checked the bus schedule, then made my way to a crowded café nearby for a cup of coffee. Now the smell of rain was unmistakable, on the waitress's blouse, even in my coffee.

I watched the streetlights flicker on one by one around the terminal as the buses came and went like giant trout cruising a mountain stream. Long lines of office workers, students, and housewives stepped up to disappear into their dark interiors. A middle-aged woman leading a black German shepherd passed in front of my window, followed by a bunch of schoolkids bouncing a rubber ball. I stubbed out my fifth cigarette and gulped the last dregs of my coffee.

I took a long look at my reflection in the window. My eyes were a bit hollow with fever. I could live with that. And my jaw was dark with five o'clock (five thirty, actually) shadow. I could live with that too. The problem was that the face I saw wasn't my face at all. It was the face of the twenty-four-year-old guy you sometimes sit across from on the train. My face and my soul were lifeless shells, of no significance to anyone. My soul passes someone else's on the street. Hey, it says. Hey, the other responds. Nothing more. Neither waves. Neither looks back.

If I stuck gardenias in my ears and flippers on my hands some people might stop and turn around. But that would be it. Three steps more and they would already have forgotten me. Their eyes saw nothing, not a damn thing. And mine were no different. I felt empty. Maybe I had nothing left to give.

Q

The twins were waiting for me.

I handed my brown shopping bag to one of them and headed for the shower. Not bothering to soap or even remove the cigarette from my mouth, I stood there under the spray and stared at the tiled wall. The bulb had been out for some time, but I could see something wander across the dark wall and disappear. It was the shadow of something I could no longer touch or summon back.

I stepped out of the shower, toweled off, and fell into bed. The coral-blue sheets were fresh and wrinkle-free. I lay there puffing on my cigarette and looking at the ceiling as the events of the day came back to me. Meanwhile, the twins were cutting vegetables, grilling meat, and boiling rice.

"Want a beer?" one of them asked.

"Yeah."

208 came to the bed with a beer and a glass.

"Music?"

"That would help."

She walked to my shelf of LPs, pulled out Handel's recorder sonatas, placed it on the turntable, and lowered the needle. My girlfriend had given it to me for Valentine's Day some years earlier. Beneath the recorder, viola, and harpsichord I could hear the sizzle of grilling meat like a basso continuo. My girlfriend and I had made love over and over while this record was playing, grinding away without a word to each other even after the music had ended and the needle crackled.

Outside the window, a silent rain fell on the golf course. I had just finished my beer and Hans-Martin Linde had just played the last note of the Sonata in F Major when dinner was ready. We had little to say to each other during the meal, which was rare for us. With no record playing, the only sounds were those of rain on the eaves and three people chewing meat. When we had finished, the twins cleared the table and made coffee. Then we sat together drinking it. The coffee smelled so good it seemed to have a life of its own. One of the girls got up to put a record on the turntable: *Rubber Soul*.

"I don't remember buying that," I called in surprise.

"We bought it!"

"We put a little money aside from what you gave us."

I shook my head in dismay.

"You don't like the Beatles?"

I bit my tongue.

"That's too bad. We thought you'd be happy."

"We're really sorry."

A twin got up to take the record off the turntable, dusting it carefully before sticking it back in its jacket. We sat there in silence. I let out a sigh.

"I didn't mean it," I apologized. "I'm just a little tired and on edge. Put it back on."

The girls gave each other a glance and giggled.

"There's no need to be polite. After all, this is your house."

"Don't worry about us."

"Please, play it again."

In the end, we listened to both sides of *Rubber Soul* with our coffee. I could feel myself calming down. The twins seemed happier too.

When we had finished the girls took my temperature. They stared long and hard at the thermometer. Ninety-nine point five, one degree higher than that morning. My head was woozy.

"That's 'cause you took a shower."

"You should go to bed."

No argument there.

I undressed and got under the covers with the *Critique of Pure Reason* and a pack of smokes. The blanket smelled of the sun and Kant was impressive as always, but the cigarette tasted like soggy newspaper on a gas burner. Shutting my book and closing my eyes, I was half tuned in to the twins' voices when the darkness dragged me down.

▶ 8

The cemetery stretched across a broad plateau near the crest of the mountain. Pathways of fine gravel crisscrossed the rows of graves, with trimmed azalea bushes scattered here and there like grazing sheep. Tall mercury lamps, curved like royal ferns, stood along the paths, casting their unnatural white light into every corner of the vast site.

The Rat had parked his car in the woods at the southeast corner of the cemetery and was sitting with his arm around the woman, gazing down at the town. At night it looked like a viscous mass of light that had been poured into a flat mold. Or a shower of gold dust deposited by some giant moth.

With her eyes closed as though she were fast asleep, the woman leaned on the Rat; he could feel her pressing against his shoulder and side. It was a strange weight. In it he could sense the fullness of a woman's existence: loving a man, bearing children, growing old and dying. The Rat pulled a pack of cigarettes from his pocket with his free hand and lit one. Now and then, an ocean breeze mounted the slope to ruffle the needles of the pines. It appeared that the woman might really have fallen asleep. The Rat brought his hand to her cheek and touched a finger to her thin lips. He could feel the moist warmth of her breath.

The cemetery looked more like an abandoned town than a graveyard. Over half the site was vacant. That was because the people who planned to be laid to rest there were still alive. Sometimes they would come with their families on Sunday afternoons to check out the grave sites they would one day occupy. Yes, a fine view, they would say, looking down at the cemetery from higher on the mountainside, flowers for every season, nice fresh air, a well-tended lawn with sprinklers—how about that!—and no stray dogs to steal the offerings. Best of all, they would think, it's a bright and wholesome place.

Satisfied, they would sit on a bench and eat their box lunches before returning to their busy lives.

The caretaker smoothed the gravel paths every morning and evening using a long pole with a plank on the end. He also chased away any children who might be after the carp in the central pond. Finally, three times a day—at nine, twelve, and six—he would play a music box version of "Old Black Joe" through the cemetery speakers. Why play music there at all? It blew the Rat's mind. Still, the darkening cemetery at six o'clock in the evening with the strains of "Old Black Joe" wafting across it was quite a trip.

The caretaker took the bus back to the world below at half past six, leaving the graveyard in total silence. Then the cars started to arrive, each bearing a couple come to make love. In summer, cars were lined up among the trees.

The cemetery held special significance for the Rat in his youth. Back in his high school days when he was still too young to drive an automobile, he had whisked up and down the riverside road time and again, always with a different girl on the back of his 250cc motorbike. He had embraced each while looking down on the same lights of town. Many sweet scents filled his nostrils, only to vanish. Many dreams, many sorrows, many promises. Yet in the end nothing remained.

You could see, if you cared to look, that death had spread its roots throughout the sprawling site. Every once in a while, the Rat would take a girl by the hand and wander along the gravel paths of the overly manicured grounds, past the graves. The names and dates of those buried beneath were written on the stones. They were the bearers of past lives, in evenly spaced rows that went on forever, like shrubs in a botanical garden.

For the dead there was no murmuring wind, no fragrance, no feelers they could extend to find their way in the dark. They were like trees cut off from time. The dead had entrusted feelings, and the words to convey them, to flesh-and-blood people. He and the girl would return to the trees and hold each other tight. The pathos of the world of the living filled everything around them, the scent of the ocean on the wind, the fragrance of leaves, the chirping of crickets in the grass.

"Did I sleep long?" the woman asked.

"No," said the Rat. "Not long at all."

▶ **9**

Each day was a carbon copy of the last. You needed a bookmark to tell one from the other.

That particular day was filled with the smell of autumn. I wrapped up work at the usual time, but when I got back to my apartment the twins were nowhere to be seen. I flopped into bed with my socks on, lit a cigarette, and let my mind wander. There were so many things I wanted to think about, but none took shape. Sighing, I sat up and glared at the white wall opposite the bed. I was stymied. Come on, man, I told myself, you can't stare at this damn wall forever. But that didn't help, either. It was what the professor who oversaw my graduation thesis told me. Good style, clear argument, but you're not saying anything. That was my problem. Now I had a rare moment alone, and I still couldn't get a handle on how to deal with myself.

It was weird. I had been on my own for years and had assumed I was getting by pretty well. Yet now I couldn't remember any of it. Twenty-four years couldn't disappear in a flash. I felt like someone who realizes in the midst of looking for something that they have forgotten what it was. What was the object of my search? A bottle opener? An old letter? A receipt? An earpick?

I gave up and grabbed my Kant from beside the bed, when a note fell from between its pages. It was written in the twins' hand. "Gone to the golf course" was all it said. This worried me. I had warned them never to go there without me. The golf course at night was not for neophytes. You never knew when a ball might come flying out of nowhere.

I put on my tennis shoes, wrapped a sweatshirt around my neck, and left the apartment. Scaling the chain-link fence, I crossed the gentle rise, skirted the twelfth hole, passed the small arbor that served as a rest stop, and cut through the woods. The setting sun split the trees on the west side of the course, splashing the fairway with light. In the dumbbell-shaped bunker near the tenth hole, I found an empty box of coffee cream cookies the twins must have left in the sand. I rolled it into a ball, stuffed it in my pocket, and stepped back to erase our footprints with my toe. Then I walked across the small wooden bridge that spanned the stream, climbed the hill, and there they were, sitting halfway up the outdoor escalator on the other side of the slope, playing backgammon.

"Didn't I tell you not to come here alone?"

"But the sunset was so pretty," one of them replied.

We descended the outdoor escalator to the field of pampas grass and sat down to enjoy the view. She had it right—the sunset was amazing.

"You shouldn't throw your garbage in the bunkers," I scolded.

"We're sorry," they chimed together.

"I got hurt once playing in the sand. Back in grade school," I said, showing them the tip of my left index finger. A tiny scar like a piece of white thread ran across it. "Someone buried a broken soda bottle in the sand."

They both nodded.

"Of course, you can't cut your hand on an empty box of cookies. But you still shouldn't throw stuff in the sand like that. It's a pure and sacred place."

"We understand," one of them said.

"We'll be careful," said the second one. "Do you have any other scars?"

"Sure I do." I showed them the whole lot. A veritable catalog of injuries. The place where a soccer ball had damaged my left eye. (The retina was still affected.) A scar near the base of my nose, also from soccer. I was heading the ball when an opponent's tooth clipped me. The seven stitches on my lower lip, from when I fell off my bike. Dodging a truck. Then there was my broken tooth . . .

We stretched out together on the cool grass, as the plumes of pampas grass rustled in the breeze.

When the last rays were gone, we headed back to the apartment for dinner. I had finished my bath and downed the last of my beer when they finished grilling the trout. There was one for each of us, with canned asparagus and a huge bunch of watercress on the side. The trout tasted like something from the good old days—a mountain path in summer. We took our time picking every last morsel from the fish with our chopsticks. All that was left on the plate was white bones and a pencil-sized watercress stalk. The twins washed the dishes right away and made coffee.

"Let's talk about the switch panel," I said. "It's been bothering me."

They nodded.

"I wonder why it's dying."

"I think it sucked in more than it could handle."

"Yeah, it just burst."

I thought for a moment, coffee cup in my left hand, cigarette in my right.

"Is there anything we can do?"

They looked at each other and shook their heads. "No, it's too late."

"It's returning to dust."

"Have you ever seen a cat die of blood poisoning?"

"No," I answered.

"At the beginning its paws and tail get hard as a rock. At the end its heart stops. It takes a long time."

I sighed. "But I hate to let it die."

"We know how you feel," one of them replied. "But it's been too hard on you."

There was nothing sentimental in their words—they could have been telling me there wasn't enough snow, so forget about skiing this winter. I gave up and drank my coffee.

▸ **10**

On Wednesday, the Rat went to bed at 9 p.m. but woke at 11. He couldn't go back to sleep. Something was squeezing his head, as if he were wearing a hat two sizes too small. An awful sensation. Giving up, he went to the kitchen in his pajamas and gulped a glass of ice water. The woman was on his mind. He stood at his window and looked down at the flashing beacon, tracing the black pier back to where her apartment stood. He remembered the pounding of the waves in the darkness, and the sound of sand whipping against her window. He was fed up with himself, and his failure to make the slightest progress, no matter how hard he tried to think things through.

Since they had begun seeing each other, the Rat's life had turned into an endless repetition—each week was identical to the last. He had lost his sense of time. What was the date? The month? October, perhaps? He had no idea . . . He and the woman got together every Saturday, and he passed the next three days, from Sunday through Tuesday, mooning over that meeting. Thursday, Friday, and half of Saturday were devoted to planning their upcoming weekend. Only Wednesday didn't fit in; it was lost in space. Unable to move forward or backward. Wednesday . . .

Ten minutes and a cigarette later, the Rat stripped off his pajamas, put on a shirt, flung a windbreaker over it, and headed down to the parking garage. It was past midnight and the town was virtually deserted, the road pitch black except for an occasional streetlight. J's Bar was already closed, but the Rat pulled the shutters up halfway, slipped underneath, and made his way down the stairs.

J had just finished hanging a dozen washed towels over the chairs to dry, and was sitting by himself at the bar, smoking a cigarette.

"Mind if I grab a beer?"

"Go ahead," J said. He sounded in a good mood.

This was the first time the Rat had visited J's Bar after hours. All the lights were off except those above the bar, and the fan and air conditioner were silent. The odor absorbed by the walls and floor hovered over the dark room.

The Rat cracked open a can of beer from the fridge behind the counter and poured half in a glass. The air felt stagnant, as if divided into several distinct layers. It was tepid and moist.

"Sorry," the Rat apologized. "I didn't plan to come tonight. But I woke up all of a sudden and really felt like a beer. I'll just drink it and split."

"Take your time," J said, folding his newspaper and brushing cigarette ash from his trousers. "If you're hungry, I'll fix you something."

"No thanks, don't bother. Beer is fine."

The beer really hit the spot. The Rat drained the glass in a single gulp and sighed. Then he poured the rest, watching the bubbles until they settled down.

"Care to join me?"

"Thanks, but I can't drink," J said, with a somewhat embarrassed smile.

"I didn't know that."

"My body can't handle alcohol. That's the way I'm built."

The Rat nodded several times, then turned his attention to his beer. It always amazed him how little he knew about this Chinese bartender. But then, J was a mystery to everyone. He never talked about himself, and when someone asked he gave only the most noncommittal answers, as if cautiously opening a desk drawer.

Everybody knew that J was a Chinese national who had been born in China, hardly unusual in a town with so many foreigners. The Rat's high school soccer team had two Chinese students on the starting squad, one forward and one defenseman. No one gave a damn.

"Some music will cheer things up," J said, tossing him the key to the jukebox. The Rat chose five tunes and came back to the counter and his beer. An old Wayne Newton song filled the room.

"Sure I'm not keeping you?" the Rat asked.

"No problem. It's not like anyone's waiting for me."

"You live alone?"

"Yeah."

The Rat pulled a smoke from his pocket, smoothed the wrinkles, and lit it.

"I do have a cat, though," J added. "She's getting on, but she's still someone to talk to."

"You talk to it?"

J nodded several times. "Yeah, we've been together so long we know each other pretty well. I can tell what she's feeling, and she's the same with me."

Cigarette between his lips, the Rat grunted, impressed. The jukebox clicked, and Wayne Newton gave way to "MacArthur Park."

"Hey, what do cats think about, anyway?"

"Lots of stuff. Just like you and me."

"Poor things," the Rat said, laughing.

J laughed too. "She's one-armed," J added after a long pause, rubbing the countertop with his fingertips.

"One-armed?" the Rat asked.

"The cat. She's a cripple. Four winters ago she came back one day all covered in blood. Her paw was smashed so bad it looked like strawberry jam."

The Rat set his beer down on the counter and looked square at J. "What happened?"

"Beats me. I thought maybe she'd been run over. But it was worse than that. A car tire can't do that to a paw. It looked as if it had been crushed with a vise. Flat as a pancake. Must have been a prank."

"No way!" The Rat shook his head several times. "Who in hell would do that to a cat?"

J tapped his unfiltered cigarette on the counter and lit it.

"You're right," he said. "No point smashing a cat's paw like that. She's a sweet cat, too, no trouble to anyone. So what's to be gained from mangling her paw? It was a senseless, evil thing to do. Still, evil like that is everywhere in this world, mountains of it. I can't understand it, you can't understand it. But it's there, no question. You could say we're surrounded by it."

With his eyes on his beer glass, the Rat shook his head one more time. "Well, it doesn't make sense to me."

"That's the best way to handle it. Admit that you don't understand and leave it at that."

J blew a cloud of white smoke into the empty room. He watched it swirl until it disappeared.

The two were quiet for a long time. The Rat studied his glass and thought his muddled thoughts, while J went on rubbing the countertop with his fingers. The last song came on the jukebox. A soul ballad, sung in falsetto.

"You know, J," the Rat said, still looking at his glass, "I've lived twenty-five years, and I don't feel like I've learned a damn thing."

J studied his fingertips for a minute. "I've been around for forty-five," he said, "and all I know is this. We can learn from anything if we put in the effort. Right down to the most everyday, commonplace thing. I read somewhere that how we shave in the morning has its own philosophy, too. Otherwise, we couldn't survive."

The Rat nodded and drained the final inch of beer from his glass. The jukebox clicked off as the last record came to an end, returning the room to silence.

"I think I get what you mean," said the Rat. He was about to say, "But," then swallowed the word. It wouldn't do any good anyway. The Rat smiled and stood up. "Thanks for the beer," he said. "Can I give you a lift home?"

"No, that's okay. I live nearby, and anyway, I like walking."

"Well, good night, then. Give my best to your cat."

"Thanks."

The Rat walked up the steps. The fragrance of cold autumn air greeted him. He tapped each of the trees lining the street with his fist as he made his way to the parking lot, where he stared for a while at the meter before getting into the car. After a moment's hesitation, he turned the car toward the ocean, stopping at a spot on the seaside road that gave him a view of the building where the woman lived. Lights were still burning in half of the apartments. He could see shadows moving behind some of the curtains.

The woman's windows were dark. Not even her bedside light was on. She must have fallen asleep already. A terrible loneliness assailed the Rat.

The sound of the waves seemed to be growing stronger. He felt as though they might overwhelm the breakwater at any moment and sweep him away, car and all, to some faraway place. He switched on the radio, clasped his hands behind his head, closed his eyes, and listened to the disc jockey's chatter. His body was so tired that those unnameable feelings had left him, having found no place to take hold. Relieved, the Rat rolled his now empty head to the side and half-listened to the waves and the DJ's voice as sleep slowly overtook him.

▸ **11**

The twins woke me up on Thursday morning. Fifteen minutes earlier than usual, but what the heck. I shaved, drank my coffee, and pored over the morning paper, so fresh from the press that its ink looked ready to smear my hands.

"We have a favor to ask," said one of the twins.

"Think you can borrow a car on Sunday?" said the other.

"I guess so," I said. "Where do you want to go?"

"The reservoir."

"The reservoir?"

They nodded.

"What are you planning to do at the reservoir?"

"Hold a funeral."

"Who for?"

"The switch panel, of course."

"I see," I said. And went back to my paper.

Unfortunately, a fine rain was falling Sunday morning. Not that I knew what sort of weather befitted a switch panel's funeral. The twins never mentioned the rain, so neither did I.

I had borrowed my business partner's sky-blue Volkswagen Beetle. "Got a girl now, huh?" he asked. "Mm," I answered. His son had smeared milk chocolate or something all over the backseat, leaving what looked like bloodstains from a gunfight. Not a single one of his cassette tapes was any good, so we spent the entire hour-and-a-half trip in silence. The rain grew stronger, then weaker, then stronger, then weaker again, at regular intervals. A yawn-inducing sort of rain. The only constant was the steady whoosh of oncoming traffic speeding by on the paved road.

One twin sat in the front passenger seat, the other in the backseat, her arms around a thermos bottle and the shopping bag that held the switch panel. Their faces were grave, appropriate for a funeral. I matched my mood to theirs. We maintained that solemnity even when we stopped to eat roasted corn. All that broke the silence was the sound of kernels popping off the cob. We gnawed the cobs bare, tossed them away, and resumed our drive.

The area turned out to be populated by hordes of dogs, who milled around in the rain like a school of yellowtail in an aquarium. As a result, I spent a lot of time leaning on the horn. The dogs showed no interest whatsoever in either the rain or our car. In fact, they looked downright pissed off by my honking, although they scampered out of the way. It was impossible, of course, for them to avoid the rain. They were all soaked right down to their butt holes—some resembled the otter in Balzac's story, others reminded me of meditating Buddhist priests.

One of the twins inserted a cigarette between my lips and lit it. Then she placed her little hand on the inner thigh of my cotton trousers and moved it up and down a few times. It seemed less a caress than an attempt to verify something.

The rain looked as if it would continue forever. October rains are like that—they just go on and on until every last thing is soaked. The ground was a swamp. It was a chilly, unforgiving world: the trees, the highway, the fields, the cars, the houses, and the dogs, all were drenched.

We climbed a stretch of mountain road, drove through a thick stand of trees, and there was the reservoir. Because of the rain there wasn't a soul around. Raindrops rippled the water's surface as far as the eye could see. The sight of the reservoir in the rain moved me in a way I hadn't expected. We pulled up next to the water and sat there in the car, drinking coffee from the thermos and munching the cookies the twins had bought. There were three kinds—buttercream, coffee cream, and maple—that we divided up into equal groups to give everyone a fair share.

All the while the rain continued to fall on the reservoir. It made very little noise. About as much as if you dropped shredded newspaper on a thick carpet. The kind of rain you find in a Claude Lelouch film.

We ate the cookies, drank two cups of coffee each, and

brushed the crumbs off our laps at exactly the same moment. No one spoke.

"Shall we?" one of the twins said at last.

The other nodded.

I put out my cigarette.

Leaving our umbrellas behind, we picked up the switch panel and marched to the end of the dead-end bridge that jutted out into the water. The reservoir had been created by damming a river: its banks followed an unnatural curve, the water lapping halfway up the mountainside. The color of the water suggested an eerie depth. Falling drops made fine ripples on the surface.

One of the twins took the switch panel from the paper bag and handed it to me. In the rain it looked even more pathetic than usual.

"Now say a prayer," one of the twins said.

"A prayer?" I cried in surprise.

"It's a funeral. There's got to be a prayer."

"But I'm not ready," I said. "I don't know any prayers by heart."

"Any old prayer is all right," one said.

"It's just a formality," added the other.

I stood there, soaked from head to toenails, searching for something appropriate to say. The twins' eyes traveled back and forth between the switch panel and me. They were obviously worried.

"The obligation of philosophy," I began, quoting Kant, "is to dispel all illusions borne of misunderstanding . . . Rest in peace, ye switch panel, at the bottom of this reservoir."

"Now throw it in."

"Huh?"

"The switch panel!"

I drew my right arm all the way back and hurled the switch panel at a forty-five-degree angle into the air as hard as I could. It described a perfect arc as it flew through the rain, landing with a splash on the water's surface. The ripples spread slowly until they reached our feet.

"What a beautiful prayer!"

"Did you make it up yourself?"

"You bet," I said.

The three of us huddled together like dripping dogs, looking out over the reservoir.

"How deep is it?" one asked.

"Really, really deep," I answered.

"Do you think there are fish?" asked the other.

"Ponds always have fish."

Seen from a distance, the three of us must have looked like an elegant memorial.

▶ 12

That Thursday morning, I wore my first sweater of the fall. It was your everyday gray Shetland fraying under the arms, but it felt great. I shaved with more care than usual and put on thick cotton pants and a pair of scuffed desert boots from my shoe cabinet. On my feet, the boots looked like a couple of trained puppies sitting at attention. The twins scoured the apartment to gather my cigarettes, my lighter, my wallet, and my commuter pass.

At the office, I sat at my desk drinking the coffee the girl had brought and sharpening my six pencils. The room was filled with the smell of wool and pencil shavings.

I ate lunch out, and then went back to the pet shop to play with the Abyssinian cats. There were two now—when I stuck the tip of my little finger through the tiny crack in the window they competed with each other to jump up and bite it.

This time, the guy running the shop let me hold them. Their fur was as soft as the finest cashmere, and the tips of their noses against my lips were cold.

"They really like people," the clerk explained.

Returning the cats to their cage, I thanked him and purchased a useless box of cat food, which he wrapped for me. As I left the shop, cat food in hand, the two cats stared at me, as if I were a fragment from their dreams.

Back at the office, the girl picked the hair off my sweater.

"I was playing with cats," I explained. I felt some sort of excuse was called for.

"Your sweater's coming apart under the arm."

"I know. It happened last year. I was holding up an armored car and caught it on the rearview mirror."

"Take it off," she said, not amused.

I took it off, and she began to mend the armpit with black yarn, her long legs crossed over the side of the chair. In the meantime I returned to my desk, sharpened that afternoon's quota of pencils, and set back to work. When all was said and done, at least no one could fault my work. I was the kind of guy who finished a set amount in a set amount of time, in as conscientious a way as possible. I bet they would have loved me at Auschwitz. The problem, as I saw it, was that the places I fit in were all out of date. Not much I could do about that, though.

I mean, it wasn't necessary to go back as far as Auschwitz and twin-seater torpedo planes. When was the last time you heard a Jan and Dean song, or saw a miniskirt? Or a woman in garters and a girdle, for that matter?

When the hands on the clock pointed to three, the girl reappeared and set my regular hot tea and three cookies on my desk. She had done a fabulous job darning my sweater.

"I'd like to ask your advice about something, if you have time."

"Sure," I said, biting into a cookie.

"It's about our trip in November," she said. "What do you think of Hokkaido?"

From the beginning, the three of us had set November as the month for our annual office trip.

"Sounds good to me," I said.

"Then it's decided. Do you think there'll be bears?"

"Bears?" I said. "No, I think they're hibernating by then."

She seemed relieved. "By the way, are you free for dinner? I know a great lobster restaurant near here."

"Sounds good to me," I said.

The restaurant was on a quiet residential street a five-minute cab ride away. No sooner had we taken our seats than a black-garbed waiter glided across the palm mat carpet to lay menus the size of paddleboards on our table. We ordered two beers to start.

"The lobster here is delicious. They boil them alive."

I grunted and sipped my beer.

Her slender fingers were fiddling with the star-shaped pendant around her neck.

"If you've got something to say, you'd better say it before the food comes," I said, then regretted it right away. It's always like that.

She smiled a very small smile. Her lips had shifted maybe a tenth of an inch and stopped, as if returning to their original position were too big a hassle. The empty restaurant was so quiet we could almost hear the lobsters' antennae moving.

"Do you like your work?" she asked.

"Like? I've never thought about my work that way, not once. No complaints, though."

"I've got no complaints either," she said, taking a swallow of beer. "The pay is good, the two of you are nice, I get regular vacations . . ."

I was all ears. I hadn't listened this closely to someone for ages.

"But I'm only twenty," she went on. "I don't want to end up this way."

We were quiet as the waiter laid out the food.

"You're still young," I said after he had left. "You'll fall in love, get married. Things will change one after another."

"No, nothing will change," she whispered, deftly removing her lobster's shell with her knife and fork. "No one will fall in love with me. I'll be darning sweaters and setting out crummy cockroach traps until I die."

I sighed. I felt, all of a sudden, that I'd aged several years.

"Look, you're cute and charming, and you've got long legs and a sharp mind. You can even shell lobsters. Things will go fine."

She fell silent and went on eating her lobster. So did I. As I ate I pictured the switch panel sitting at the bottom of the reservoir.

"What were you doing when you were twenty?"

"I was stuck on a girl." Nineteen sixty-nine—the time of our life.

"What happened?"

"We split up."

"Were you happy?"

"Looking back, I guess I was," I said, swallowing another mouthful. "Just about anything looks better from a distance."

The restaurant had filled up by the time we finished our lobster, the clatter of forks and knives and the squeak of chairs making a lively racket. I ordered coffee, while she ordered coffee and lemon soufflé.

"How about now?" she asked. "Is there anyone special?"

I thought for a moment before deciding to leave out the twins. "No," I answered.

"Aren't you lonely?"

"I'm used to it. I trained myself."

"Training? What sort?"

I lit a cigarette and aimed the smoke at a spot two feet above her head. "I was born under a strange star. Like I've always been able to get whatever I want. But each time something new comes into my hands, I trample something else. Follow me?"

"A little."

"No one believes me, but it's the truth. It hit me about three years ago. So I decided. Not to want anything anymore."

She shook her head. "And do you plan to live like that forever?"

"Probably. Then I won't hurt anyone."

"In that case," she said, "you ought to live in a shoe box."

A pretty cool way to look at it, if you ask me.

·   ·   ·

We walked to the station side by side. My sweater was perfect for the evening air.

"Okay," she said. "I'll try to figure things out."

"Sorry I couldn't be more help."

"Just talking about it takes a load off my mind."

Our trains were leaving from the same platform, heading in opposite directions.

"Sure you're not lonely?" she asked one more time. I was still trying to come up with a good answer when the train arrived.

▸ **13**

On any given day, something can come along and steal our hearts. It may be any old thing: a rosebud, a lost cap, a favorite sweater from childhood, an old Gene Pitney record. A miscellany of trivia with no home to call their own. Lingering for two or three days, that something soon disappears, returning to the darkness. There are wells, deep wells, dug in our hearts. Birds fly over them.

What grabbed me that Sunday evening in October was pinball. The twins and I were sitting on the eighth green of the golf course, watching the sunset. The eighth hole is a par five, with no obstacles to speak of. Just a long fairway straight as an elementary school hallway. We were watching the evening sun sink behind the hills, while in the background a student who lived nearby was practicing scales on his flute, a heartrending sound. Why did pinball snatch my heart at that particular moment? I have no idea.

As time went on, my mental image of pinball grew and grew. If I closed my eyes I could hear the sounds of balls striking bumpers, scoreboards churning out numbers.

Q

I wasn't that into pinball back in 1970, when the Rat and I were spending all our time drinking beer in J's Bar. The bar had one machine, a model called Spaceship, unusual for its time in that it had three flippers. The lower cabinet was divided into two playfields, with one flipper on the upper half and two below. It was a model from a peaceful era, before the world of pinball was inflated by solid-state technology. The Rat, however, was a true fanatic; he got me to snap a commemorative photo of him and the pinball machine on the day he reached his all-time high score of 92,500. It shows him leaning against the machine, grinning from ear to ear, while beside him the machine is grinning too, proud of the score on its display. The one and only heartwarming snapshot I took with my Kodak pocket camera. The Rat looks like a Second World War flying ace, the pinball machine like an old fighter plane. The sort of plane that started when a mechanic spun its propeller, and whose windscreen was snapped down by the pilot after takeoff. The number 92,500 linked the Rat and the machine, making them look almost like blood brothers.

The pinball company sent someone to J's Bar once a week to collect the money and service the machine. He was about thirty, a gaunt man of few words. Avoiding J's eyes, he would move straight to the Spaceship, remove the panel underneath with his key, and direct the jangling stream of coins into a canvas utility bag. Having completed that task, he would insert one of the coins to start the machine, snap the plunger a few times, and then shoot a ball out onto the playfield in a bored sort of way. With that single ball he checked the magnets on all the bumpers, tested all the lanes, and knocked down the targets one by one. The drop target, the kick-out hole, the rotating target. Next, he set off all the bonus lights and then wrapped up the job by dispatching the ball into the exit drain with a look of complete disinterest. Then he left, nodding at J on his way out the door to let him know everything was in order. All in less time than it takes to smoke half a cigarette.

It was a dazzling display that left the Rat and me gaping: ash was hanging from the tip of my cigarette, while the Rat's beer was entirely forgotten.

"It's like a dream," said the Rat. "If I had technique like that I could hit 150,000 easy. No, 200,000 is more like it."

"Don't beat yourself up," I consoled him. "He's a pro." But the pride of the ace pilot was gone, never to return.

"Compared to him I've gotten about as far as holding a woman's pinky," the Rat said, before clamming up. Yet I could see he was still lost in pointless dreams of six-digit scores.

"That's his job," I tried to persuade him. "It might be fun at first. But try doing it from morning till night, day after day. Anybody would get sick of it."

"No," said the Rat, shaking his head. "I wouldn't."

▸ **14**

J's Bar was packed for the first time in ages. Most were new faces, but J had no problem with that—a customer was a customer. It felt as if the summer rush had come round again: the sound of the ice pick, the tinkle of ice against glass, the laughter, the Jackson 5 on the jukebox, clouds of white smoke billowing against the ceiling like comic-strip balloons.

For the Rat, though, something had changed. He sat alone at the corner of the bar with an open book in front of him, reading the same page over and over again until he gave up and closed the cover. What he really wanted to do was gulp down the rest of his beer and head back to his apartment to sleep. That is, if *true* sleep was in the cards.

For a week, the Rat had felt forsaken, abandoned by everything, including luck itself. He was living on beer, cigarettes, and catnaps. Even the weather was crappy. Rain had washed soil from the mountainside into the river, turning the ocean into a patchwork of brown and gray. A depressing sight. He felt as if his head were stuffed with balled-up old newspapers. Sleep, when it came, was brief and shallow. It was like being in an overheated dentist's waiting room: every time the door opened, he woke up and looked at the clock.

Midway through the week, during a bout of solitary whiskey drinking, the Rat decided to shut down his thought processes for a while. One by one, he packed each rift in his consciousness with ice thick enough to hold the weight of a polar bear. Convinced that would get him through the rest of the week, he rolled over and went to sleep. When he woke up, though, everything was the same. Except that now his head hurt a little.

The Rat stared at the six empty bottles lined up before him with bleary eyes. J's back was visible between the cracks.

Maybe it's time to retire, the Rat thought. I was eighteen when I had my first beer in this bar. Since then there have been thousands of beers, thousands of orders of French fries, thousands of records on the jukebox. Like waves lapping the sides of a barge, they've all come and gone. Haven't I already drunk enough beer? Of course, I can drink buckets' worth in my thirties and forties too. But still, he continued, the beer I drink *here* is different . . . Twenty-five, not a bad age to call it quits. A sensible person would have finished college and be employed as a loan officer in a bank.

The Rat added another empty bottle to the lineup and drained half of his too-full glass in a single swallow. By reflex, he wiped his mouth with the back of his hand. Then he wiped his wet hand on the seat of his cotton pants.

Okay, he said to himself, let's go through this again, no copping out halfway this time. Twenty-five . . . a time to crack down and do some serious thinking. Add two twelve-year-old kids together and you get the same age. Are you worth as much as they are? Hell, one of them counts more than you. A pickle jar full of ants counts more than you . . . Screw these stupid metaphors! They don't help a damn bit. Think: you slipped up somewhere. Where? Try to remember . . . How the hell can I?

The Rat gave up and drained his glass. He signaled for a new bottle.

"You're hitting it too hard," J said. But bottle number eight showed up anyway.

His head was sore. His body was rising and falling like a boat on the waves. He could feel a weight behind his eyes. Time to throw up, said a voice inside his head. Puke first, then you can think. Okay, then, let's head to the restroom . . . Shit! I can't even make it to first base . . . Nevertheless, the Rat pulled himself together enough to walk to the restroom, kick out the girl who was reapplying her eyeliner in the mirror, and crouch over the toilet.

How many years since I last threw up? How do I do it? Do I take off my pants? . . . Enough with the crummy jokes. Shut up and puke. Puke your guts out.

The Rat puked his guts out, sat down on the toilet, and lit up a smoke. When he finished, he washed his face and hands with soap and straightened his hair in the mirror with his wet hands. His face was a little morose, but his features weren't all that bad. Probably good enough to catch the eye of a junior high school teacher.

When he left the restroom, the Rat made a beeline for the girl with the half-penciled-in eyebrows and apologized. Back in his seat at the counter, he drank half a glass of beer and drained the ice water J set before him in a single gulp. Then he shook his head two or three times and lit a cigarette, at which point his mind began to work again.

Okay, let's get it in gear, he said aloud. The night is long—enough time to figure it all out.

▶ **15**

I entered the occult world of pinball for real in the winter of 1970. Looking back, it was as if I spent the next six months living at the bottom of a dark hole. I dug a hole just my size in the middle of a meadow, squeezed myself in, and blocked my ears to all sound. Nothing outside held the slightest appeal. When evening rolled around I woke up, slipped on my coat, and headed for the game arcade.

It took a while, but I finally located a three-flipper Spaceship identical to the one at J's Bar. When I slipped in my coins and pushed Play, a string of notes sounded, as if the machine were quivering with anticipation. Ten targets popped up, the bonus light went off, the score flipped back to six zeroes, and the first ball hopped into the chute. For exactly one month, I poured buckets of coins into the slot. Then one cold and rainy early-winter evening, like a hot air balloon jettisoning its last sandbag, I cracked the six-figure barrier.

Tearing my trembling fingers from the flipper buttons, I leaned against the wall, sipped my freezing can of beer, and stared for a long time at the six numbers on the scoreboard—105,220.

That moment marked the beginning of my brief love affair. I more or less gave up on school and spent the bulk of the money from my part-time job on pinball. I mastered the techniques— hugging, passing, trapping, the stop shot—so well that before long spectators gathered when I played. At times high school girls in bright red lipstick would rub their soft breasts against my arm as I pressed the buttons.

The worst of winter had just arrived when I passed the 150,000-point mark. Almost no one was left in the freezing game arcade, but I continued to soldier on in a heavy duffel coat with a scarf hiked up to my ears. I was glued to the machine. The face I saw in the restroom mirror every so often was skeletal, the skin dry and flaky. I would take a break every three games to lean my shivering body against the wall and drink a beer. The last swallow always tasted like lead. Cigarette butts scattered around my feet, I would pull a hot dog from my pocket and gnaw on it.

But she was marvelous. The three-flipper Spaceship . . . only I understood her, and only she truly understood me. Each time I pressed Play, she sang that gratifying melody, flipped her board to six zeroes, and smiled at me. I coolly pulled the plunger back to the perfect spot, not a millimeter off, and launched the gleaming silver ball up the chute and out into her playfield. Watching it bounce around, I felt as free as if I had smoked a pipe of the finest hashish.

Many thoughts flitted in and out of my head, like disconnected fragments. People appeared in the glass atop her field, then disappeared. Like a magic mirror of dreams, the glass reflected my mind, growing brighter and darker in tandem with the flashing bumpers and bonus lights.

It's not your fault, she said to me. She shook her head several times. *Not your fault at all. You did what you could.*

You're wrong, I said. Left flipper, tap transfer, Target 9. *All wrong. I didn't do a damn thing. Didn't lift a finger. I could have done something if I'd set my mind to it.*

You humans can only do so much, she said.

Maybe so, I said. *But it's not over. It'll be like this forever.* Return channel, trap, kick-out ball, rebound, hugging, Target 6 . . . bonus light. 121,150. *It is over,* she said. *Over and done with.*

She disappeared in February. The game arcade was razed, and by the following month an all-night doughnut shop stood in its place. The kind of joint where girls in gingham uniforms serve dry doughnuts on plates with a similar pattern, and patrons— the high school kids whose motorbikes are lined up outside, the night cabbies, the die-hard hippies, the bar girls—all look bored as they drink their tasteless coffee. I ordered a cup of that hideous concoction and a cinnamon doughnut and tried to find out if my waitress knew anything about the game arcade.

She looked at me with suspicious eyes. The way she would regard a doughnut that had fallen on the floor.

"Game arcade?"

"Yeah, the one that was here until a little while ago."

"No idea," she said with a sleepy shake of her head. Whose memory went back a month? It was that kind of neighborhood.

I walked the streets, my mood black. No one knew what had become of the three-flipper Spaceship.

So I gave up pinball. Everybody does when the time comes. That's all there is to it.

▸ 16

On Friday evening the rain that had been falling for days lifted without warning. The town had absorbed so much water that, from the Rat's balcony window, it appeared bloated. The setting sun had broken through the clouds, turning them a strange color and dyeing the inside of his apartment.

The Rat slipped a windbreaker over his T-shirt and headed down the slope. The black pavement was dotted with puddles as far as the eye could see, the air heavy with the odor that follows an evening rain. Droplets showered from the green needles of the waterlogged pines that lined the river. Brown runoff poured down the river's banks and slid along its concrete bottom toward the sea.

The evening glow soon gave way to a spreading, sodden cloak of darkness. Then, in an instant, the moisture turned to fog.

With his elbow hanging from his car window, the Rat slowly cruised through town. The white fog was moving west, through the hilly residential district. In the end he turned down the river road to the ocean. He pulled in beside the breakwater and lit a cigarette. Everything was black and wet: the beach, the massive concrete blocks protecting the shore, the trees that blocked the sand. An inviting yellow light was filtering through the blinds of the woman's apartment. The Rat checked his watch. Seven fifteen. A time when people were finishing their meals and melting into the snug warmth of their homes.

The Rat put his hands behind his head, closed his eyes, and tried to picture the woman's apartment. He had been there just twice, so his memory was shaky. When you first came in the door there was a kitchen, about ten feet square . . . an orange tablecloth, pots of leafy plants, four chairs, orange juice, a newspaper on the table, a stainless steel teapot—all in its place, all spotless . . . Farther in was a room that had once been two small rooms, the divider having been removed. It contained a long, narrow desk with a glass top, and on that . . . three ceramic beer mugs. They were stuffed with all sorts of things—pencils, rulers, drafting pens. On a tray were erasers, a paperweight, ink remover, old receipts, adhesive tape, paper clips of many colors . . . a pencil sharpener and postage stamps.

To the side of the desk were a well-used drawing board and a desk lamp with a very long neck. The lamp shade was . . .

green. The bed was straight ahead, against the far wall. A small Scandinavian model made of unpainted wood. It creaked like a rented rowboat when they were on it.

The fog was getting thicker with each passing moment, a milky darkness creeping across the beach. Now and then a car crawled past the Rat, its yellow fog lamps illuminating the road in front of him. The fine mist from the open window had soaked everything inside: the seats, the windshield, the Rat's windbreaker, the pack of cigarettes in his pocket. The foghorns on the ships anchored at sea were emitting sharp, plaintive wails, like calves that had strayed from the herd. Some of the wails were brief, others long, but each had its own distinct pitch as it cut through the darkness on its way toward the mountains.

And on the wall on the left? The Rat continued to remember. A bookcase, a portable stereo, and records. A chest for clothes. Two prints by Ben Shahn. A modest array of books in the bookcase. Most had to do with architecture. Then there were travel books, guidebooks, travelogues, maps, a few best-selling novels, a biography of Mozart, sheet music, several dictionaries . . . a French dictionary with an inscription of some kind written inside the front cover. Most of the records were either Bach, Haydn, or Mozart. Also a few relics from her girlhood . . . Pat Boone, Bobby Darin, the Platters.

After that the Rat was stymied. Something was missing. Something important. Without it the room would remain floating in space, detached from reality. What was it? Okay, hold on a sec . . . I remember. The lighting and . . . the carpet. What sort of lights? What color carpet? . . . For the life of him he couldn't remember.

The Rat was seized by the impulse to jump out of his car, cut through the trees, and knock on her door just to find out. Idiot! He sat back again and looked at the ocean. Nothing was visible except the white fog covering the dark sea. Deep within the fog, the beacon's orange light flashed on and off, as repetitive and reliable as a beating heart.

The woman's apartment floated in the dark for a while, minus its ceiling and floor. Then, one by one, its details faded until it had disappeared completely.

The Rat looked up at the roof of the car and slowly closed his eyes. As if flipping off a switch, he extinguished the remaining lights in his head and descended into a new sort of darkness.

▸ 17

The three-flipper Spaceship . . . her voice was calling me from somewhere. It went on like that day after day.

I sped through the work piled on my desk at a tremendous clip. I gave up my lunch breaks and stopped playing with the Abyssinian cats. I spoke to no one. The girl came to check on me every so often, then left shaking her head, appalled. I completed my day's work by two o'clock and hightailed it out of there, tossing the completed manuscripts on her desk as I passed. My destination was the game arcades of Tokyo, my purpose the quest for the three-flipper Spaceship. But the quest proved fruitless. No one I met had seen or even heard of the machine.

"Wouldn't the four-flipper Journey to the Center of the Earth do?" asked one arcade owner. "We just got one in."

"No, it wouldn't. Sorry."

He appeared a little disappointed.

"Then how about the three-flipper Southpaw? Hit for the cycle and you get a bonus ball."

"Sorry. I'm just interested in the Spaceship."

Still, he was kind enough to give me the name and telephone number of a pinball enthusiast he knew.

"This guy may know something about what you're looking for," he said. "He's what they call a catalog junkie. Knows more about pinball machines than anyone. Bit of a weirdo, though."

"I owe you one," I said.

"No sweat. Hope you find it."

I went into a quiet coffee shop and dialed the number. A man picked up after five rings. He spoke softly. I could hear NHK's seven o'clock news and a crying baby in the background.

I told him my name. "It's about *a certain machine*," I said, getting right to the point.

His end of the line went silent for a few moments.

"What machine might that be?" he said. The television sound had been lowered.

"The three-flipper Spaceship."

I could hear him thinking.

"There's a planet and a spaceship on the back cabinet—"

"I'm familiar with it," he cut me off. He cleared his throat. "That model was launched by the Chicago company Gilbert and Sands in 1968." His tone was that of a university lecturer fresh out of graduate school. "Some call it the machine of misfortune."

"Machine of misfortune?"

"How about it?" he said. "Let's get together—maybe we can work something out."

Our meeting was set for the following evening.

We exchanged business cards and ordered coffee from the waitress. I was amazed to discover he was in fact a university lecturer. He looked a bit past thirty and his hair was thinning, but he was tan and well built.

"I teach Spanish," he said. "It's like sprinkling water in the desert."

I nodded, dutifully impressed.

"Does your translation agency handle Spanish?"

"I look after the English and another guy takes care of French. That's all we can handle."

"How disappointing," he said, arms still folded. He didn't look disappointed, though. He fiddled with the knot of his tie for a few moments.

"Ever been to Spain?" he asked.

"No such luck," I said.

The coffee came. We drank it in silence, with no more talk of Spain.

"The firm Gilbert and Sands came late to the world of pinball," he said, breaking into his lecture. "From the Second World War right through the Korean War, their primary business was manufacturing bomb-delivery systems, but when the fighting stopped they took the opportunity to embark on a new path, what we call the peace industries. Pinball machines, bingo machines, slot machines, jukeboxes, popcorn vending machines—you name it, they made it. Their first pinball machine was completed in 1952. Not a bad job, either. It was very durable and cheap. But it didn't spark people's interest. To quote the review in *Billboard* magazine, it had all the sex appeal of a Soviet Women's Corps government-issue brassiere. Still, from a business point of view it was a success. The machine was exported to Mexico, then to other Central American nations. Countries short on specialized technical know-how. They were happy to get sturdy machines that didn't need the servicing more complicated models required."

He took a sip of water. I could tell he regretted not having an overhead projector and a long pointer.

"Nevertheless, as you know, the pinball business in the United States, and by extension the world, was dominated by the companies known as the Big Four—Gottlieb, Bally, Chicago Coin, and Williams. Gilbert and Sands tried to force their way into this oligopoly, which led to a spirited, five-year-long battle. In the end, in 1957, Gilbert pulled out."

"Pulled out?"

Nodding, he drank what remained of his coffee, grimaced, and dabbed at his mouth with his handkerchief.

"Yes—they were defeated. They still made money, though. From their Central American exports, you see. But they decided to get out before the bleeding got too bad . . . Manufacturing and maintaining pinball machines is a terribly complex operation. It requires a team of seasoned, specialized technicians, and planners to lead them. You also need to build a nationwide service network: agents who can supply parts when necessary and enough repairmen to reach a broken machine within five hours. Gilbert didn't have the clout to operate on that scale. So they swallowed their disappointment and withdrew, shifting their resources to things like vending machines and windshield wipers for Chrysler automobiles. That went on for about seven years. But they never abandoned their plans for pinball."

Here he came to a halt. He drew a cigarette from his jacket

pocket, tapped it a number of times on the table, and lit it with a lighter.

"No, they hadn't given up. A matter of pride, I guess. They threw a big chunk of money into a secret factory for pinball research and covertly recruited Big Four retirees for their project team. The team's orders were as follows: within five years, build us a pinball machine that can compete with the Big Four. That was in 1959. They took full advantage of those five years, so that by the end they had used their other products to establish a network that stretched all the way from Vancouver to Waikiki. With that their preparations were complete.

"They rejoined the game right on schedule in 1964 with their new model. The Big Wave."

He pulled a black scrapbook from his leather briefcase, opened it, and handed it to me. In it were pasted what appeared to be magazine clippings, including a photograph of the Big Wave, diagrams of its playfield and board design, and even a play guide.

"It's a unique machine, in fact, packed with all kinds of ingenious devices never seen before. Take the sequence pattern, for example. The Big Wave allowed you to set it to fit your own level of skill. People ate it up.

"Of course Gilbert's innovations are all old hat now, but at the time they were startling. The machine was also constructed in a very conscientious way. First of all, it was durable. The Big Four were turning out machines built to last about three years, but the Big Wave was built to last for five. Second, it emphasized technique, reducing luck's role in the outcome . . . Gilbert later produced a number of other great machines along the same lines. The Orient Express, Sky Pilot, TransAmerica—

all praised to the skies by those in the know. Spaceship was the last model they released.

"Spaceship was radically different from its predecessors. The four machines that preceded it had been all about novelty, while Spaceship was extremely orthodox and simple. None of its mechanisms varied from what the Big Four were already using. In that sense, you could say it was a defiant gesture. They felt they no longer had to take a backseat to anyone."

He was speaking slowly and distinctly, as if to a student. I nodded again and again as I sipped my coffee, and when that was finished, my water. When that was gone I smoked a cigarette.

"Spaceship was an enigma. At first glance there seemed to be nothing special about it. But that changed the minute you began to play. It had the same flippers as the other machines, the same targets, yet something about it was different. Whatever that something was, it captivated people's minds, like opium. Why, I don't know . . . There are two reasons I call Spaceship the machine of misfortune. First, no one grasped its true beauty. By the time they started figuring that out, it was too late. Second, its maker went bust. Gilbert was just too conscientious, I guess. So they got swallowed up by a conglomerate. That company saw no need to continue the pinball operation. End of story. That's why Spaceship is known as the phantom masterpiece: few have actually played it, even though fifteen hundred were produced. The going price in the United States now is two thousand dollars, but Spaceship fans never get a chance to pick one up."

"Why not?"

"Because nobody will let one go. They can't. It's a real enigma."

With his lecture complete, he checked his watch, a habit of his, and lit a cigarette. A second round of coffee arrived.

"How many machines were exported to Japan?"

"I looked into that. Three."

"Not very many."

He nodded. "That's because Japan wasn't part of the distribution network Gilbert had set up. In 1969 an importer brought a small number to Japan on a trial basis. Those three. By the time he decided to increase the order, Gilbert no longer existed."

"Do you know where those three machines are?"

He stirred sugar into his cup for a long time and scratched his ear.

"One ended up in a small game arcade in Shinjuku. That arcade shut down two winters ago. The machine's whereabouts are unknown."

"I'm familiar with that case."

"Another went to a game arcade in Shibuya. That place burned down last spring. Fire insurance paid for everything, though, so no one lost out. Other than the fact that one more Spaceship was lost to the world . . . The more I think about it, the more fitting 'machine of misfortune' seems."

"Kind of like the Maltese Falcon."

He nodded again. "But I have no idea where the third machine went."

I gave him the address and telephone number for J's Bar. "It's not there anymore, though. He got rid of it last summer."

He jotted down the information in his notebook as though recording a message from on high.

"The machine I'm interested in is the one in Shinjuku," I said. "Can you find out what happened to it?"

"There are several possibilities. Most often, machines are sold for scrap. The turnover is very rapid. A machine depreciates in three years, so it makes more sense to get a new one than it does to pay for repairs. Not to mention the role that fashion plays. So they're scrapped . . . The second possibility is that someone might have picked it up secondhand. Old models that are still usable frequently end up in small bars, where they spend their last days being pawed by drunks and amateurs. The third possibility is that a collector might have picked it up. That's very rare, though. Eighty percent of the time they go for scrap."

I gave myself over to dark thoughts, an unlit cigarette between my fingers.

"Regarding the last possibility, is there any way to check?"

"I could try, but it would be difficult. Fellow enthusiasts have no way to contact each other. No registers, no bulletins . . . But we can still give it a try. I have some interest in Spaceship myself."

"I'm deeply grateful."

He settled in his chair and puffed on his cigarette.

"Tell me," he said. "What was your best score on Spaceship?"

"165,000."

"That's something," he said without changing his expression. "Really something," he repeated, scratching his ear again.

▸ **18**

I spent the whole next week in an oddly peaceful and quiet mood. Pinball was still ringing in my ears, but it was faint, not like before, when it was like the mad buzzing of a dying bee in a pool of winter sunlight. As autumn deepened, piles of dry leaves mounted up beneath the trees that surrounded the golf course. They were being burned here and there on the gentle suburban slopes; from our window we could see slender plumes of smoke rising straight into the air, like magic ropes.

Gradually, the twins were becoming a little less talkative, a little more meek. We took walks, drank coffee, listened to records, and slept entwined under a layer of blankets. On Sundays we strolled to the botanical garden an hour away to munch on mushroom and spinach sandwiches under the oaks. The sharp cries of black-tailed birds rang from the treetops.

Since the air was growing chilly, I picked up two new sport shirts and gave them to the girls together with two of my old sweaters, so 208 and 209 were replaced by olive-green turtleneck and beige cardigan. The twins did not complain. Then I went out and bought them socks and new sneakers. I felt like Santa Claus.

The October rains were a treat. Cotton soft and fine as needles, they soaked the withered golf course. This time, though, the earth absorbed every drop, leaving no puddles behind. The groves were filled with the fragrance of wet fallen leaves; in the late afternoon, sunlight filtered through the trees, dappling the ground. Birds cut across the forest paths like runners in a race.

My days in the office were almost as pleasant. The work crunch had ended, so I smoked cigarettes and listened to tapes of classic jazz musicians like Bix Beiderbecke, Woody Herman, and

Bunny Berigan as I worked, pausing every other hour for a shot of whiskey and a cookie or two.

Only the girl was busy, checking timetables, making plane and hotel reservations, and, as if that weren't enough, mending two more of my sweaters and replacing the old metal buttons on my sport coat with new ones. She had changed her hairstyle and shifted to pale pink lipstick and thin sweaters that called attention to her breasts. She had begun to blend with the autumn air too.

A wonderful week that lulled us into believing things might stay that way forever.

▶ **19**

The Rat found it nearly impossible to tell J he was leaving town. For some reason, the idea was eating him up. Three nights running he went to the bar, and all three nights he left without raising the subject. Each time he tried to say the words, his throat turned bone dry and he had to drink a beer. Then he would have another, and another, until he was overcome by an unbearable sense of futility. Damn it, he thought, what is the point of struggling like this? Where is it getting me? Nowhere.

When the clock pointed to twelve, the Rat gave up and, with a certain sense of relief, said his usual good-night to J and left the bar. The evening breeze had turned cold. He went back to his apartment, sat on the bed, and turned on the TV. Then he opened a can of beer and lit a cigarette. There was an old Robert Taylor western, commercials, the weather report, more commercials, and finally white noise . . . The Rat turned off the

TV and took a shower. Then he had another can of beer and smoked one more cigarette.

Where would he go once he left town? No destination presented itself.

For the first time in his life, he felt real dread. Black and glistening it was, like a mass of eyeless, pitiless worms creeping up from the bowels of the earth. They wanted to drag him down, back to where they had come from. Their slime oozed through his body. He cracked open another can of beer.

By the end of those three days the Rat's apartment was filled with empty cans and cigarette butts. He missed the woman like crazy. His whole being longed for her warmth. He wanted to enter her and stay there. Yet he could never go back. Face the music, he told himself. You're the one who burned the bridges. You're the one who plastered the walls and sealed yourself inside, right?

The Rat looked down at the flashing beacon. The sky was starting to brighten, turning the ocean gray. Then, at the very moment the darkness was swept away by the clear morning sunlight like a tablecloth yanked from a table, the Rat fell into bed and slept—his pain, with no other place to go, stretched out beside him.

The Rat's determination to leave the town had once seemed unshakable. He had taken a long time to arrive at that decision, thought it through from every conceivable angle. Having ensured that there were no cracks in his reasoning, he had lit a match and torched the bridges, sending all the attachments he had to the place up in flames. Sure, a few traces of himself might

stick around. But no one would care. As the town kept changing, those remnants would eventually vanish . . . Everything
would follow its prescribed course.

And then there was J.

The Rat couldn't figure out why J's existence bothered him
so much. It should be simple, he thought; just walk in, tell him
I'm leaving town, and wish him the best. It wasn't as if they
were best buddies—they hardly knew anything about each
other. In the end they were just two passing strangers who had
chanced to meet. So why this pain? The Rat lay on his bed and
punched the air with his fist.

It was just after midnight on Monday when the Rat lifted the
shutters of J's Bar and slipped underneath. As usual, J had
turned off half the lights and was sitting at a table, smoking a
cigarette. When he saw the Rat come in he smiled and nodded.
In the gloom, J looked strangely old. A shadow of black stubble
covered his cheeks and jaw, his eyes were sunken, and his thin
lips were dry and cracked. Veins stood out in his neck, and his
fingertips were yellow with nicotine.

"Feeling tired?" the Rat asked.

"Yeah, a little," J said. He fell silent for a moment. "It's one of
those days. We all have them."

The Rat nodded and pulled up a chair.

"There's a song that says, 'Rainy days and Mondays always
get me down.'"

"They got that right," J said, staring at his fingers holding
the cigarette.

"You should hurry home to bed."

"To hell with that," J said, shaking his head. He shook it slowly, as if shooing away a bug. "Doubt I'll be getting much sleep tonight anyway."

By reflex, the Rat glanced at his watch. Twelve twenty. The gloomy basement was dead quiet—time itself seemed to have died. With the shutters down, not a shred was left of the sparkle the Rat had sought there for so many years. Everything was faded and bone tired.

"Could you bring me a Coke?" said J. "Grab a beer for yourself while you're at it."

The Rat stood up and went to the fridge, returning with the drinks and two glasses.

"How about some music?" J asked.

"Not tonight," said the Rat. "Let's keep it quiet."

"Feels like some kind of funeral."

The Rat laughed. They sat there drinking the Coke and the beer in silence. The ticking of the Rat's watch on the table was almost deafening. Twelve thirty-five, yet it felt as if they had been there for ages. J barely moved. The Rat watched J's cigarette burn down in the glass ashtray until the butt turned to ash.

"Why are you so tired?" the Rat asked.

"Why?" J shifted his crossed legs as if he had just remembered to move them. "No special reason, I guess."

The Rat downed half his beer and returned the glass to the table with a sigh.

"You know, J. Everyone's rotting, correct?"

"True enough."

"And there are many ways to rot," the Rat went on, wiping his mouth with the back of his hand. "But I think each individual's choices are really limited. We can choose between only a couple of ways—two or three at the most."

"You could be right."

What was left of the Rat's beer sat in the bottom of his glass like a puddle of water, the bubbles gone. He pulled a crumpled pack from his pocket, drew out a cigarette, and put it to his lips. "But I've come to believe it doesn't really make a damn bit of difference. One way or the other, we're all going to rot. Don't you think?"

J just listened, holding his glass of cola at an angle.

"Yet people keep changing. For the longest time, I couldn't figure out what the point was." Chewing on his lip, the Rat stared at the table in thought. "So here's my conclusion. Whatever changes they go through, whatever progress they make, in the end it's only a step on the road to decay. Am I wrong?"

"No, I don't think you're wrong."

"That's why I couldn't care less about anyone who happily trots along toward the void . . . Or this whole friggin' town, for that matter."

J said nothing. The Rat did the same. He took a match from the box on the table, struck it, and watched the flame burn down the shaft before lighting his cigarette.

"The problem is," said J, "*you* are about to make a change. Am I right?"

"Dead on."

Neither spoke for a few seconds. Ten seconds, perhaps. It was J who broke the silence.

"People are awkward creatures. A lot more awkward than you seem to realize."

The Rat emptied the last of his beer into his glass and downed it in a single gulp. "I'm lost."

J nodded.

"It's hard to know what to do."

"I figured that much." J smiled. The talking seemed to have tired him out.

The Rat slowly stood up and stuffed his cigarettes and lighter in his pocket. The clock said it was already past one.

"Good night," the Rat said.

"Good night," said J. "Hey, here's something someone once told me: Walk slowly, and drink lots of water."

The Rat smiled at J, opened the door, and headed up the stairs. The street was brightly lit and totally deserted. He sat down on the guardrail and looked up at the sky. So then, he thought, how much water do I have to drink?

▸ 20

The Spanish instructor telephoned during lunch the Wednesday after the November holidays ended. My partner had gone to the bank, and I was in the kitchen eating the spaghetti our office girl had whipped up. She had boiled it about two minutes too long and had substituted finely chopped *shiso* for basil, but it still tasted good. We were in the midst of a serious discussion about the art of cooking spaghetti when the phone rang. She picked up the receiver, but after a few words, she shrugged and handed it to me.

"I'm calling about Spaceship," he said. "I've located it."

"Where?"

"It's a bit difficult to say over the phone," he said. A moment of silence followed.

"By which you mean?" I asked.

"I mean it's hard to explain on the phone."

"Like I won't believe it until I've seen it?"

"No," he said after a pause. "It'd be hard even if it were sitting right in front of you."

I couldn't think of a response, so I waited for him to go on.

"Look, I'm not blowing this out of proportion, and I'm not joking, either. We simply have to meet."

"Sure thing."

"How about this afternoon at five?"

"Fine with me," I said. "Will I get to play?"

"Of course," he said. I thanked him and hung up. Then I dug back into the spaghetti.

"Where are you going?"

"To play pinball. I'm not sure where."

"Pinball?"

"Yeah. You know, hitting balls with flippers."

"Of course I know. But why pinball?"

"Why? This world is rife with matters philosophy cannot explain."

She put her elbows on the table, propped her chin in her hands, and thought for a moment.

"Are you good at pinball?"

"I used to be. It was the only thing I could really take pride in."

"I've got nothing like that."

"Then you've got nothing to lose."

While she pondered that one, I ate what remained of my spaghetti and helped myself to a ginger ale from the fridge.

"There can be no meaning in what will someday be lost. Passing glory is not true glory at all."

209

"Who said that?"

"Can't recall. But I agree with the idea."

"Is there anything in this world that can't be lost?"

"I believe there is. You should too."

"I'll do my best."

"Maybe I see the world through rose-colored glasses. But I'm not as big a fool as I seem."

"I know that."

"I'm not bragging—I just think being an optimistic fool beats the alternative."

She nodded. "So that's why you're off to play pinball this evening."

"You got it."

"Stick up your hands."

I raised my arms to the ceiling while she inspected the armpits of my sweater.

"Okay," she said. "Have a good time."

Ⓠ

I met the Spanish instructor at the same coffee shop as before, and we piled into a taxi without delay. Straight down Meiji Avenue, he told the cabbie. Once we were moving he pulled out a pack of cigarettes, lit one, and offered me one as well. He was wearing a gray suit and a blue necktie with three diagonal stripes. His shirt was blue too, though somewhat paler than the tie. I had on a gray sweater, jeans, and my scuffed desert boots. I felt like a failing student summoned to his professor's office.

When we passed the Waseda Avenue intersection the cabbie asked if we were going much farther. Turn on Mejiro Avenue, the instructor said. A moment later we did.

"Is it very far?" I asked.

"Pretty far," he answered, fumbling for another smoke. I looked out my window at the shops passing by.

"Our machine was damn hard to find," he said. "I started by running down my list of pinball fanatics, one by one. I contacted the whole lot, not just in Tokyo but across the country, all twenty of them. But I didn't come up with anything. None of them knew any more than we do. Next, I made the rounds of the dealers who handle used machines. There aren't many. But the total number of transactions is huge. Getting them to work through their lists was a real pain."

I nodded and watched as he lit his cigarette.

"Thank goodness we knew the approximate date. February 1971, right? I told them to focus on that time frame. And they found it! Spaceship, maker Gilbert and Sands, serial number 165029, February 3, 1971, tagged for disposal."

"Disposal?"

"Scrap. Crushed in a compactor, like in *Goldfinger*. Turned into a cube of metal to be recycled or dumped offshore."

"But you said . . ."

"Let me go on. Anyway, I thanked the dealer and went home. I figured it was a lost cause. But something deep inside kept nagging me. Call it intuition. He was wrong, said this little voice. It wasn't like that. So the next day I returned to the same dealer. And then I went from his office to the scrap yard. I watched them work for half an hour, went into the office, and gave my card to the guy at the desk. A university lecturer's business card does wonders with people who don't know what we do in reality."

He was speaking somewhat faster than the first time we had met, which made me a little uncomfortable.

"I manufactured a story—told him I needed to learn more about the scrap business for a book I was writing.

"He was willing to cooperate. But he couldn't recall any pinball machines from February 1971. That was natural: two years had passed, and there's no way he can track everything he handles. All he does is put the stuff together, toss it in the compactor, and wham! So I asked him one last question. If I saw something I wanted—say a washer or a bike frame—that was about to be scrapped, would he sell it to me if the price was right? Sure, he said. And are there ever cases like that?"

The autumn dusk had swiftly faded and the road was sinking into darkness. Our taxi was approaching the suburbs.

"He told me I should check with the supervisor on the second floor if I needed more detailed information. Of course I went up and asked. Did he know anyone who might have picked up a pinball machine around February 1971? Yes, he answered, I know one such person. When I pressed him for details, he gave me the man's telephone number. It seems this guy is called when any machines come in. He slips the supervisor some money for the privilege. And how many had he bought up? I asked. That's hard to say offhand, he said. The guy looks over each one; then he takes it if he likes it and leaves it if he doesn't. A ballpark estimate is okay, I said. I don't need a specific number. Well, he said, I'm sure he's picked up at least fifty machines."

"Fifty machines!" I cried.

"You got it," the lecturer said. "That's the man we're going to see."

▸ **21**

Outside it had turned pitch black. Not a monochromatic but a layered black, as if various black paints had been slapped on like butter.

I sat with my nose to the taxi window looking out. As time passed, the black came to appear somehow flat, as if someone had taken a razor to matter without substance, and the darkness was the severed end. The result was a most odd perspective, at once three-dimensional and two-dimensional. A giant night bird with outspread wings rose before me.

The farther we drove, the more scattered the houses became, until all that was left were fields and groves of trees, from which arose the rumbling of a million insects. Low-lying clouds hung over the landscape like giant boulders while the creatures cowered, silent in the dark. Only the bugs retained their voice.

The Spanish instructor and I took turns smoking cigarettes without exchanging a word. The cabbie was smoking too, as he scowled at the passing headlights. My fingers drummed on my knee. From time to time, I had the urge to open the cab door and flee.

Switch panels, sandboxes, reservoirs, golf courses, torn sweaters, pinball—how long would this go on? I sat there bewildered, clutching my random assortment of cards. I wanted to turn around that very instant and head home. Take a nice bath, crack open a beer, grab my cigarettes and my Kant, and climb into my warm bed.

So why was I racing through the darkness? To keep a date with fifty pinball machines. It was idiotic. A dream. A dream without substance.

Yet the siren call of the three-flipper Spaceship never wavered.

Q

We were five hundred yards off the road in the middle of an empty field when the Spanish instructor told the cabbie to stop. The ground was level, with soft grass that brushed our ankles like river water in the shallows. I got out of the cab, stretched, and took a few deep breaths. I could smell chickens nearby. No lights were visible, but the faint illumination from the road brought the landscape into dim relief. The buzz of countless insects surrounded us. They seemed ready to drag me down somewhere by my feet.

We stood there, waiting for our eyes to adjust to the dark.

"Is this still Tokyo?" I asked after a long pause.

"Of course. Where did you think we were?"

"It looks like the edge of the world."

The Spanish instructor nodded gravely. The fragrance of grass and the smell of chicken shit enveloped us as we smoked our cigarettes in silence. The smoke rolled along the ground like smoke from a signal fire.

"There's a chain-link fence over there." He pointed into the dark as if shooting a pistol on the practice range, his arm extended straight from his side. I could make out something fencelike if I strained my eyes. "Follow it for three hundred meters and you'll hit the warehouse."

"Warehouse?"

"Yes," he said, without glancing in my direction. "It's a big building—you can't miss it. It used to be cold storage for chicken carcasses. But it's not in use anymore. The chicken company went broke."

"But I still smell chickens."

"Smell chickens . . . ? Ah yes. Their smell soaked into the soil. It's even worse when it rains. You can almost hear flapping wings."

Nothing was visible inside the chain-link fence. It was a frightening darkness. Even the insects sounded suffocated.

"The warehouse is unlocked. The owner left the door open for you. The machine you're looking for is inside."

"Have you been in there?"

"Only once . . . He was kind enough to let me take a look," he said. I could see the orange tip of the cigarette between his teeth bobbing in the dark. "The light switch is to your right as you enter. Watch out for the stairs."

"Aren't you coming?"

"Go in alone. That's the deal."

"The deal?"

"That's right," he answered, extinguishing his butt in the grass with his foot. "You're welcome to stay as long as you wish. Just turn off the lights on your way out."

The air was growing colder every minute. A blanket of chill rose from the ground.

"Have you met the owner?"

"Yes," he answered after a short pause.

"What kind of man is he?"

The instructor pulled a handkerchief from his pocket and blew his nose. "Nothing special about him," he said with a shrug. "At least on the outside."

"Then why would he go out and buy fifty pinball machines?"

"Listen, there are all kinds of people in this world. It's that simple, I guess."

I doubted it was that simple. But I thanked him anyway and headed off along the chicken plant's chain-link fence. No, not that simple at all, I thought. There was a slight difference between collecting fifty pinball machines and, say, fifty wine labels.

The warehouse looked like an animal crouching in the dark. Tall grass grew thick around its base, and its gray walls were windowless. A gloomy, foreboding structure. Above the double steel doors a name, probably that of the company, had been daubed over with white paint.

I stood ten paces away and looked at the building. The more I thought, the less likely it seemed that I would come up with any good ideas, so I walked to the entrance and gave the ice-cold doors a push. They swung open into a darkness completely different from the one I had been experiencing.

▸ **22**

I found the wall switch in the dark and flipped it on. A few seconds later, fluorescent ceiling lights blinked into action, bathing the warehouse in white light. There must have been at least a hundred lights in all. The warehouse was bigger than it looked from the outside, but even so, the cumulative brilliance of all those fluorescent bulbs forced me to close my eyes. When I opened them again, the darkness was a distant memory—only the silence and the chill remained.

The warehouse resembled the inside of a giant refrigerator, which made sense given its original purpose. The ceiling and windowless walls had been painted a glossy white, but they were covered with stains, some black, some yellow, and some like no color I had seen before. I could tell right away the walls were very thick. It was like being stuffed in a lead box. I kept glancing back at the door, fearful that, somehow, I might be trapped there forever. Surely no building had ever been designed to create a more disagreeable feeling.

Viewed in a charitable light, it could have been an elephant graveyard. But instead of white skeletons with folded legs, there were endless rows of pinball machines spread across the concrete floor. I looked down at this strange sight from the top of the steps. My hand crept to my lips, then returned to my pocket.

There were lots and lots of pinball machines. Seventy-eight, to be precise. I knew this because I counted, several times. Seventy-eight, beyond a doubt. They all faced the same direction in eight columns that stretched to the far wall of the warehouse. The columns were precise, as if following chalk lines on the floor. Like flies suspended in acrylic resin, the machines were frozen in time. Seventy-eight deaths, seventy-eight silences. My instinctive reaction was to start moving. Otherwise, I might be inducted into this company of gargoyles.

It was cold. And the smell of dead chickens was everywhere.

I slowly descended the five steps of the narrow concrete staircase. It was even colder at the bottom. Yet I was sweating. A nasty sweat, too. I took a handkerchief from my pocket and mopped my face, but there was nothing I could do about the sweat pooling under my arms. I sat on the bottom step and lit a cigarette with shaking hands. This was not the way I wanted to meet the three-flipper Spaceship. And I was sure this wasn't the way she preferred to meet me . . . pretty sure, anyway.

By closing the door, I had shut out all the insect voices. A perfect silence blanketed the floor like a heavy fog. The seventy-eight pinball machines stood rooted to the floor on their three hundred and twelve legs, tons of metal with nowhere to go. It was a pitiful sight.

I tried whistling the first four bars of "Jumpin' with Symphony Sid" from my seat on the step. Stan Getz and his head-shaking, foot-tapping rhythm section. My whistling resounded throughout the cavernous warehouse—I thought it sounded beautiful. Somewhat revived, I whistled the next four bars. Then the four after that. I could feel every thing around me pricking their ears to my tune. Of course, they didn't shake their heads or tap their feet. My whistling died away, sucked into the far corners of the warehouse.

"Damn, it's cold," I muttered, after running through the whole song. The echo didn't sound like me at all. It flew up to the ceiling before swooping down to settle like mist on the floor. I sighed, the cigarette still in my mouth. I couldn't sit there forever doing my one-man show. If I didn't move, the cold and the chicken stink would penetrate my core. I stood up and brushed the cold dirt off my trousers. Then I crushed my cigarette with my shoe and tossed the butt into a tin can close by.

Pinball . . . pinball. Wasn't that why I had come? The cold seemed to be paralyzing my brain. Think! About pinball. About the seventy-eight machines . . . Okay, consider the switch. There has to be an electric switch somewhere in the building that can return all seventy-eight machines to life. Look for the switch.

With my hands in the pockets of my jeans, I shuffled along the wall of the cavernous room. Torn electrical wiring and severed lead pipes dangled from the naked concrete, remnants of the days when the building was used for cold storage. Holes gaped where the various meters, junction boxes, switches, and other machines had been located, as if they had been ripped out by brute force. Up close, the wall was slimier than it had appeared from a distance. Like the trail left by a giant slug. As I walked, I realized how enormous the building was. Not your usual chicken-packing plant.

At the far end of the floor was a staircase like the one I had just walked down with an identical steel door at the top. It was easy to imagine that I had walked in a full circle back to where I had started. I tried pushing the door open, but it didn't budge. It had no lock or bolt, but there was an absolute lack of movement, as if it had been glued shut. I withdrew my hand from the door and wiped my sweaty face. My hand smelled like chickens.

The switch was next to the door. A big lever. The moment I pulled it, a deep growl filled the room, a spine-chilling sound that seemed to rise from beneath the earth. Next came an immense flapping of wings, as if tens of thousands of birds had taken to the air at once. I wheeled around to look at the warehouse floor. The noise came from thousands of numbers flipping back to zero in unison as the seventy-eight machines drank in the electricity. Once they finished, all that remained was a dull hum, like a swarm of bees. The sound of seventy-eight pinball machines, restored to life if only for a moment, filled the warehouse. Primary-colored lights flashed on every playfield, while the boards on the back cabinets competed to assert their individual dreams.

I descended the steps and strolled through the columns like an officer reviewing his troops. A few of the machines were vintage models I had only seen in photographs, while others I remembered with fondness from arcades of the past. Still others were remembered by no one, machines lost in time. There was Friendship 7, released by Williams—who was the astronaut featured on its board? Glenn . . . ? That would have been from the early '60s. There was Bally's Grand Tour, with its blue sky, Eiffel Tower, and happy American tourists. Gottlieb's Kings & Queens, the model with eight rollover lanes. It featured a Western Gambler with a manicured mustache, a nonchalant expression, and an ace of spades tucked in his suspenders.

Superheroes, monsters, college girls, football players, rockets, women—so many dreams left to fade and rot in darkened game arcades. Now they were all smiling at me from their boards. And the women . . . Blondes, platinum blondes, brunettes, redheads, Mexican girls with raven hair, ponytailed girls, Hawaiian girls with hair to their waists, Ann-Margret, Audrey Hepburn, Marilyn Monroe . . . each thrusting out her glorious breasts from beneath diaphanous blouses unbuttoned to the waist, or one-piece bathing suits, or pointy bras . . . Their colors would fade, but their breasts would retain their eternal beauty. The lights flashed on and off as if in time with the beating of my heart. The seventy-eight pinball machines were a graveyard of old dreams, old beyond recall. I walked slowly past those dream women.

The three-flipper Spaceship was waiting for me at the end of the line. She stood there, a picture of serenity, sandwiched between her gaudy sisters. She could have been seated on a flat stone in a forest clearing. I stood before her, gazing with fondness at her familiar board. The blue of her cosmos, so deep and dark it looked like poured ink. The tiny white stars. And the planets: Saturn, Mars, Venus . . . A pure white spaceship floated in the foreground. Lights burned in its windows, inviting you to imagine the happy family moments being shared inside. Shooting stars arched across the night sky.

The field was just as I remembered. The same dark blue. The targets were pure white, like teeth flashing through smiling lips. The ten lemon-yellow bonus lights, stacked to resemble stars, pulsing up and down. Saturn and Mars, the two kick-out holes, and Venus, the rotating target—taken together, the epitome of peace and tranquillity.

Hey there, I said. Well, maybe I didn't say it out loud. But I placed my hands on the glass surface of her field. It was as cold as ice. When I removed my hands, their warmth left ten cloudy fingerprints. Awakened at last, she smiled at me. How I had missed that smile. I smiled back.

It feels like ages since I last saw you, she said. I pretended to add up the time on my fingers. Three years, I replied. Gone in a heartbeat.

We silently nodded at each other. We might have been sipping coffee in a café, toying with the lace curtains.

I think of you a lot, I said. It gets me feeling pretty low.

When you can't sleep?

Yes, when I can't sleep, I parroted. Her smile never wavered.

Aren't you cold? she asked.

Yes, I'm cold. Freezing, actually.

Don't stay too long. This place is too cold for you.

Seems so, I answered. My hands were trembling as I withdrew a cigarette from my pocket, lit it, and inhaled the smoke.

Want to play? she asked.

No thanks, I replied.

Why not?

My top score was 165,000. Remember?

Of course I remember. It was *my* best score too.

So I don't want to spoil the memory, I said.

She didn't speak. Only her ten bonus lights continued to pulse up and down. I studied the ground as I smoked my cigarette.

Why did you come?

I heard you call.

Call? She seemed confused for a moment; then she smiled a bashful smile. Yes, you may be right. I may have called you.

I looked for you everywhere.

Thanks, she said. Talk to me.

There have been a lot of big changes, I said. Your game arcade became an all-night doughnut shop. Their coffee is the pits.

Is it really that bad?

It looks like the muddy water the dying zebra drinks in that old Disney flick.

She laughed softly. She was a real knockout when she smiled. But that was an awful neighborhood, she said, her face growing serious. Everything was so crude, so filthy . . .

It was like that everywhere back then.

She nodded. So what are you doing now?

I'm a translator.

Fiction?

No, I said. Scum. I scoop it from one ditch and dump it into another one, that's all.

Is it fun?

Fun? I've never thought of it in those terms.

Do you have a girlfriend?

You may not believe me, but I'm living with twins right now. They make really great coffee.

She looked off into space, the sweet smile playing on her lips. It feels strange somehow, she said. Like none of it really happened.

Oh, it happened all right. But now it's gone.

Does it make you sad?

No, I said, shaking my head. There was something that came out of nothing, and now it's gone back to where it came from, that's all.

We fell silent again. What we shared was no more than a fragment of a time long dead. Yet memories remained, warm memories that remained with me like lights from the past. And I would carry those lights in the brief interval before death grabbed me and tossed me back into the crucible of nothingness.

You'd better go now, she said. For sure, the cold was becoming harder to bear. I was shivering all over as I stubbed out my cigarette.

Thanks for coming to see me, she said. We may not meet again, but take care of yourself.

Thanks, I said. So long.

I passed between the columns of pinball machines, climbed the steps, and threw the switch. The machines fell silent, like balloons emptied of air. Silent and asleep. I walked the length of the warehouse once again, mounted the steps, turned off the lights, and shut the door behind me. Not once in all that time did I look back. Not once.

Q

By the time I hailed a cab and returned to the apartment, it was almost midnight. The twins were in bed, finishing the crossword puzzle from a weekly magazine. I was as white as a sheet and reeked of frozen chicken. I threw my clothes in the washing machine and hopped in the bath for a long soak. After thirty minutes in the hot water I felt ready to rejoin the human race, but that didn't get rid of the icy cold that had seeped into my core.

The twins pulled the gas heater out of the closet and turned it on. It took fifteen minutes for me to stop shaking; then, after a short break, I ate a hot bowl of canned onion soup.

"I'm all right now," I said.

"For real?"

"You still feel cold," the other twin said, frowning, her hand on my wrist.

"I'll be warm in a minute."

The three of us climbed into bed and worked out the last two words of the crossword. One was "trout," the other "stroll." I warmed up in no time, and none of us knew who fell asleep first.

I saw Trotsky's four reindeer in my dream. They were all wearing thick wool socks. It was an awfully cold dream.

▸ 23

The Rat never saw the woman after that. Nor did he return to observe the light in her apartment. In fact, he avoided going anywhere near her building. Something had floated up in the pitch black of his heart like a wisp of white smoke from a blown-out candle and then disappeared. A dark silence followed. Silence. When you stripped something down layer by layer, what remained in the end? The Rat didn't know. Pride? . . .

He lay on his bed and studied his hands. It seemed that no one could live without pride. If that was all one had left, though, it was too dark. Way too dark.

Breaking up had been easy. He simply hadn't phoned the woman one Friday evening. He guessed that she had stayed up late waiting for the call. The thought pained him. Time and again he had to hold himself back from reaching for the telephone. He put on his headphones and turned up the volume on his record player. He knew she wouldn't phone, but even so he didn't want to hear it ring.

She had probably waited until midnight before giving up. Then she would have washed her face, brushed her teeth, and gone to bed. Maybe he'll phone tomorrow morning, she'd have thought as she turned out the lights. But the phone would not ring Saturday morning, either. She would open the windows, make breakfast, water the potted plants. She wouldn't give up on his call for good until the afternoon. Then she would brush her hair and smile a few times in the mirror, as if practicing. Oh well, she would think, this is the way it was bound to end.

The Rat spent all that time in his room with the blinds pulled down, staring at the hands of the electric clock on the wall. The air never moved. From time to time he lapsed into a light and fitful sleep. The clock no longer signified anything. The darkness grew thicker and lighter by turns—that was all. The Rat could feel his body losing its substance, its weight, its sensations, but he bore with it. How long have I been like this, he wondered. How many hours? The white wall facing him wavered with each breath. Space grew dense, and began to invade his body.

When he judged he could stand it no longer, the Rat took a shower and shaved, still in a daze. Then he toweled himself off and drank a glass of orange juice from the refrigerator. When he had finished, he changed into fresh pajamas and went back to bed. Well, that's the end of that, he thought. This time he fell into a deep sleep. A terribly deep sleep.

▸ **24**

"I'm leaving town," the Rat told J.

It was six in the evening, and the bar had just opened. The counter was waxed, the ashtrays emptied of butts and scrubbed clean. The rows of liquor bottles were wiped and shining with their labels facing out, while a neat arrangement of sharply creased napkins, Tabasco sauce bottles, and salt shakers perched on each of the little trays. J was whipping up bowls of three different salad dressings. The smell of garlic hung in the air like a fine mist. That quiet moment before the customers arrived.

The Rat had borrowed J's nail clippers, and was trimming the fingernails of his left hand, dropping the clippings into one of the ashtrays.

"Leaving? To go where?"

"Nowhere in particular. Someplace new. A small town probably."

J funneled the salad dressing into three large flasks. When he finished, he stuck the flasks in the refrigerator and wiped his hands.

"What'll you do there?"

"Find a job," the Rat said, carefully inspecting his fingers.

"What's wrong with this place?"

"Not an option," said the Rat. "I sure would like a beer."

"It's on me."

"Thanks a million."

The Rat took his time pouring the beer into a frosted glass. "Aren't you going to ask why this town doesn't do it for me?" he asked after draining half the glass in one gulp.

"I think I know already."

The Rat laughed and clicked his tongue. "See, J, it doesn't work," he said. "The way everyone pretends to be on the same wavelength without questioning or talking about things—it doesn't get anyone anywhere. I hate to say it, but . . . I feel like I've been hanging around that kind of world too damn long."

"You could be right," J said after some thought.

The Rat took a sip of beer and began working on the fingernails of his right hand. "I've given it a lot of thought. And I know the situation may be no different wherever I go. But I still have to leave. If it turns out to be the same, I can live with it."

"Think you'll ever come back?"

"Of course I will. Someday. It's not like I'm running away from anything."

The Rat took a few peanuts from the small bowl, opened them with an audible crack, and tossed their wrinkled shells in his ashtray. He took his napkin and wiped away the condensation his cold beer had left on the paneled counter.

"So when do you leave?"

"I don't know. Maybe tomorrow, maybe the day after. Within the next three days anyway. I'm all packed."

"It's really sudden."

"I know. Sorry to have been such a pain in the ass."

"Hey, a lot of things have gone down." J nodded several times as he dusted the rows of glasses on the sideboard with a dry cloth. "But when it's over, it all seems like a dream."

"I guess you're right. But you know it'll probably take me a hell of a long time to really feel that way."

J paused for a moment.

"Yeah," he laughed. "I know. I forget sometimes there's twenty years between us."

The Rat poured what remained of his beer into his glass and sipped it. He had never drunk a beer so slowly before.

"Want another?"

The Rat shook his head slowly. "No, I'm good. I planned this as my last beer. The last one *here*, I mean."

"So you're not coming again?"

"No, that's part of the plan. It'd be too rough."

J laughed. "We'll meet again."

"Next time you may not recognize me."

"I'll recognize your smell."

The Rat took a long last look at his trimmed fingernails, stuffed the uneaten peanuts into his pocket, wiped his mouth with the napkin, and left the bar.

The wind flowed soundlessly, as if sliding through an invisible rift in the darkness. It rustled the tree branches overhead, dislodging their leaves, which made a faint, dry sound as they hit the car roof. After dancing about, they skated down the windshield to pile on the fenders.

The Rat sat alone in his car among the cemetery trees, staring through the windshield. Language had deserted him. A few meters ahead the land fell away. Beyond was dark sky and ocean; below, the lights of the town. He was slouching forward, both hands on the steering wheel, his eyes fixed on a single point in the sky. Though his body was motionless, the tip of the unlit cigarette in his fingers described complex yet meaningless patterns in the air.

Breaking the news to J had left him with an unbearable empty feeling. It seemed as if, all of a sudden, the various rivulets that formed his consciousness, barely holding him together, had headed off in different directions. Could they find each other again? The Rat had no idea. Those dark streams would eventually reach the boundless sea. With luck, they might meet there, but . . . had his twenty-five years been lived for this? He couldn't answer his own question. It was a good question, though. The good ones never had answers.

The wind was growing stronger. It caught the faint warmth rising from humanity and carried it far away, leaving behind only the cold darkness and the countless glittering stars. The Rat removed his hands from the steering wheel. He played with the cigarette between his lips for a while; then, as if remembering, he lit it.

His head throbbed. It was a strange sensation, not so much pain, more like cold fingertips pressing on his temples. He shook his head to drive his thoughts away. Whatever, he concluded. It's all over now.

He pulled his road atlas from the glove compartment and leafed through it. He tried reciting some of the place names in order. Most were small towns wholly unfamiliar to him. They followed the roadways in an interminable line. After reading a few pages, he felt the fatigue that had built up over the past few days crash down on him like a towering wave. A lukewarm sludge oozed through his veins.

He longed to sleep.

Sleep would wash everything away. If he could just sleep . . .

When he closed his eyes he could hear the winter surf striking the seawall and threading its way between the concrete blocks of the breakwater back to the open sea.

At least I don't have to explain myself to anyone anymore, thought the Rat. How much more warm and peaceful and quiet the bottom of the sea might be than any of those towns. But enough thinking. Enough.

▸ 25

The hum of pinball machines had vanished from my life. Ditto the thoughts with no place to go. There would be no Knights of the Round Table–like grand finale, of course. That was still far away. From now on, I vowed, when my horse was exhausted, my sword broken, and my armor rusty, I would lay myself down in a meadow of green foxtail and listen to the wind. I would follow the path I should follow wherever it took me, whether that be the bottom of a reservoir or a chicken plant's refrigerated warehouse.

I know the following brief epilogue will seem trivial, of no greater consequence than a clothesline in the rain.

But here goes.

One day the twins came home from the supermarket with a box of cotton swabs. Three hundred swabs packed in one carton. After that they took to cleaning my ears when I finished my bath, one on each side. They were very good at it. I would close my eyes and drink beer and listen to the swabs whisper in my ears. One night, however, I happened to sneeze halfway through. And in that second, I lost almost all my hearing.

"Can you hear me?" asked the one on the right.

"Only a little," I said. My voice seemed to be coming from behind my nose.

"How about me?" said the one on the left.

"Same thing."

"It's your fault for sneezing," said one.

"Yeah," said the other. "That was dumb."

I sighed. It was as if I had bowled a seven-ten split, and both pins were nattering at me.

"Will drinking water help?" asked one.

"Fat chance," I shouted angrily.

Nevertheless, they forced me to drink a whole bucket of water. All that did was make my stomach ache. But my ears didn't hurt, which I took to mean that the force of the sneeze had driven the earwax farther inside. That was the only theory that made sense. I located two flashlights in the closet and had them check. Like two spelunkers in a cave, they beamed their lights in my ears for several minutes.

"I don't see anything."

"Clean as a whistle on this side."

"Then why the hell can't I hear?" I shouted again.

"Your ears have given up the ghost."

"You're deaf."

Ignoring them, I found the ear, nose, and throat clinic nearest to us in the telephone book and gave them a call. Talking on the phone was no easy matter in my condition, but the nurse sounded sympathetic. Come right away, she said. We'll leave the front door open. The three of us threw on our clothes, raced out the door, and followed the bus route to the clinic on foot.

The doctor was a woman in her fifties with hair like tangled barbed wire, but she struck me as a nice person. Opening the waiting-room door herself, she stopped the twins' chattering with a clap of her hands, sat me down in a chair, and listened to my story with a bored look on her face.

I get the picture, so for goodness' sake stop shouting, she said when I finished. Then she took a huge syringe, filled it with an amber liquid, and handed me something like a tin megaphone to place beneath my ear. She inserted the syringe and pushed the plunger, whereupon the amber liquid went galloping merrily into my ear like a herd of zebras before overflowing into the megaphone. This was repeated three times, after which she probed the ear with a slender cotton swab. When she had treated both ears in this manner I could hear as well as before.

"I can hear!" I said.

"Earwax," she responded tersely. It sounded like that children's word game where you turn the last syllable of one word into the first syllable of the next.

"But we couldn't see it."

"Because of the curve."

"The curve?"

"Your ear canals are a lot more curved than other people's."

She sketched my inner ear for me on the back of a matchbox. It was bent at a right angle, like a bookshelf bracket.

"So you see, if earwax goes around that bend, you can call it all day and it will never come back."

"So what can I do?" I groaned.

"Do? Just be careful cleaning your ears. *Careful.*"

"Are there further consequences if your ear canals are especially bent?"

"Further consequences?"

"Like for example . . . psychological ones?"

"None," she said.

We added an extra fifteen minutes to our walk home by cutting across the golf course. The dogleg on the eleventh hole reminded me of my inner ear, the flag of a cotton swab. And that wasn't the end of it. The clouds crossing the moon became a squadron of B-52s, the thick stand of trees in the west a fish-shaped paperweight, the stars moldy parsley flakes . . . you get the idea. Anyway, my ears were now attuned to the sounds of this world to a splendid degree. It was as if a veil had been stripped away. I could hear things taking place miles away: the cries of night birds, people shutting their windows, other people talking of love.

"What a relief," said one twin.

"Thank goodness," said the other.

Tennessee Williams once wrote: "So much for the past and present. The future is called 'perhaps,' which is the only possible thing to call the future."

Yet when I look back on our dark voyage, I can see it only in terms of a nebulous "perhaps." All we can perceive is this moment we call the present, and even this moment is nothing more than what passes through us.

That was pretty much what I was thinking when I said good-bye to the twins for good. I was silent the whole way across the golf course, as we went to catch the bus two stops down the road. It was a Sunday morning and the sky was a piercing blue. The grass beneath our feet was filled with the premonition of its approaching death until the next spring. Before long it would turn white with frost, and then disappear beneath a blanket of snow. The snow would glitter in the crystal-clear morning sunlight. The pale grass crunched beneath our feet as we walked along.

"What are you thinking?" one of the twins asked me.

"Nothing," I said.

The twins were wearing the sweaters I had given them and carrying their sweatshirts and a change of clothing in paper bags under their arms.

"Where will you go?" I asked them.

"Back where we came from."

"Yeah, we're just going back."

We passed the sand trap and the eighth hole's straight-as-an-arrow fairway, and walked down the outdoor escalator. A big flock of small birds was sitting on the grass and the chain-link fence, watching us go by.

"I can't say this very well," I said. "But I'm really going to miss you both."

"We're going to miss you too."

"We'll be lonely."

"But you're going, right?"

They nodded.

"And you're sure you have someplace to go?"

"Of course," said one.

"If we didn't, we wouldn't go back," said the other.

We climbed over the fence, cut through the trees, and there was the bus stop. We sat on the bench to wait for the bus. On a sunny Sunday morning, the stop was quiet and peaceful. We sat there in the light and played the children's word game together. Five minutes later the bus arrived, and I gave them money for their fares.

"See you around," I said.

"See you around," said one.

"See you around," said the other.

The phrase echoed in my heart for a long while.

The bus doors closed with a bang, and then they were waving to me from the window. Everything repeats itself . . .

I retraced the path we had taken back to my apartment, put the *Rubber Soul* record they had left me on the turntable, made some coffee, and sat there in the autumn light, watching the rest of that Sunday pass by outside my window. A November Sunday so tranquil it seemed that everything would soon be crystal clear.

1969–1973

A NOTE ABOUT THE AUTHOR

Haruki Murakami was born in Kyoto in 1949 and now lives near Tokyo. His work has been translated into more than fifty languages, and the most recent of his many international honors is the Jerusalem Prize, whose previous recipients include J. M. Coetzee, Milan Kundera, and V. S. Naipaul.

A NOTE ON THE TYPE

The text of this book was composed in Apollo, the first typeface ever originated specifically for film composition. Designed
by Adrian Frutiger and issued by the Monotype Corporation of
London in 1964, Apollo is not only a versatile typeface suitable
for many uses but also pleasant to read in all of its sizes.

Composed by North Market Street Graphics, Lancaster, Pennsylvania
Printed and bound by Berryville Graphics, Berryville, Virginia
Designed by Maggie Hinders